Urban Townes

Urban Townes

Bruce Double'u

2010

I

Liza Maine watched her new, young boyfriend walk the old, bare hallway towards the kitchen. He had offered to get her mom a beer. He was new to their house and walked gingerly on the tile floor, his basketball shoes popping twice from the slightly sticky floor. Liza remembered being slightly embarrassed about the house; inviting him over; her alcoholic mom; the bare walls; the same worn and run-down carpeting in the living room that covered the same stairwell for as long as she and her two sisters and one brother could remember. She remembered the sudden annoyed nervousness of not wanting to introduce them to each other once he had arrived; the early change of heart; the formalities that—for the first time—began to seem a bit ludicrous. Liza realized, even then, that she had arranged an internal confessional for her own benefit. She had wanted to show somebody how she lived and why she was, pretty sure, she had to get out. At least that was what her older brother and sister had done. They had moved out. They had their own places on the other side of town. Her brother had a bachelor pad and her sister did not have a live-in boyfriend. But, they had moved-on. They were doing what they were supposed to do. Right down to night classes at the local Community College.

Liza never did pride herself on her memory but she felt she had a good one. As she got older she seemed to remember very clear snapshots of things and certain events. Like thinking about the few boyfriends she had asked to 'come over' and see her house and, maybe, meet her mother. Warren. Norman. Joshua. Joshua had been the 'first'—the cherry popper. And he had made that perfectly clear to his hockey friends, and it had been somewhat embarrassing for Liza to deal with as a sophomore in High School. And Joshua was a senior, at the time, and graduated to a State College to earn a hockey scholarship but earned a felony statutory rape charge instead. Apparently the girl had lied about attending the University. Liza would eventually wonder if the girl had been lying or, at the least, exaggerating the legalities of her story. Liza could not help but wonder, often, about the allegation. Maybe she had lied. Liza thought she had known Joshua well. But, she rarely spoke to Joshua after that. Liza would normally laugh at herself when she began to think about the past too much. But Joshua's story was different. Liza, occasionally, would have a difficult time deciding if Joshua had gotten what he deserved or was a victim of circumstance. Liza recalled seeing Joshua, once, on Christmas break. And Joshua had been unceremoniously discharged the following semester. They had one, last brief conversation over the phone:

"It's not as bad as you think." Joshua had said.

"No?" Liza was only 17. It seemed pretty clear with the law and a rape charge involved. Liza wondered little why she had not been more promiscuous in high school. She had been saving herself...And then Joshua. She realized she was not thinking anything terribly new here. After all, it has always been a fine line for teenage girls becoming women not to be perceived as a 'slut' or a prude. But, when looking back, Liza could see these boys as clear as the day it happened. Surprised how she had thought she was in love, so easily, with Joshua the first. Surprised how it had hurt her in so many different ways; sexually and emotionally. A fool to believe, so simply, she thought she knew what was right and wrong? She felt like she realized how cruel, unsure, and insecure boys could be while trying to remain confident and in control.

Liza did not think Joshua had been that rough with her, initially. But, it had been her first time and would cause her to reassess their time together; in the car or at his house when nobody was home as 'quickly' as possible. It made her think, sometimes, more than she liked.

"How old is she?" Liza had asked.

"I don't know...she said she was a student here."

"You'd just met her?" And when Joshua had taken a long time to answer Liza remembered thinking it did not matter. She basically said she had to go and hung-up the phone on the kitchen wall. That was basically the last time she had spoken with Joshua; and the lingering finality of their relationship.

Liza was still in High School when she stumbled upon the inevitable fear of becoming like her mother. It was the first time she had really thought "My God, my mother looks old." Her parents divorced when Liza was a High School freshman and her mom did not stop drinking for about three years. When Liza's new boyfriend handed her mom the non-alcoholic beer Liza could not help but blurt out the truth.

"Honey, you didn't have to tell him I'm an alcoholic...."

Liza had been surprised by the sound of her own voice. The remark resounded a brutal honesty that Liza wished she could have taken back. But she never did apologize. What good would it have done to apologize for stating a fact even if it did sound cruel? Liza laughed at herself, sometimes, for thinking about such things, years later. It seemed so trivial but she could not help her basic instinct. Her basic, a priori instinct that was probably inherited from her parents: to be nice to people. Growing up she had never looked to tease or create an uncomfortable, social situation. Liza thought she knew quite a few people who thought and lived just the same way. If she had a style when she was 15, 16, and 17- that was it: friendly, blonde, and smiling; and never considered a bimbo.

Some classmates were surprised to find out she was on the school swim team; and quite competitive. She had been proud of her improvement especially in the backstroke. She even partied less during swim season. She had never drank much—for obvious reasons, she thought—but she liked to smoke her 'reefer'; the 'chronic' as Liza and her closer friends used to call their playful little addiction.

The summer after graduation had become a blur. It was probably a self induced, smoky haze. The last 'blowout' before everyone she knew continued with their lives. She could still see the faces; the expressions of some of her friends who did not know how to answer.

"Will we see each other...?" Liza was more surprised now why she cared so much then. And she did not like to remember feeling sad about graduating from High School. It made her feel childish. Her friends had been nothing more than moral and social stepping stones who seemed to take their growth and departure well. Still.

Liza laughed at herself less these days along with the snapshots of her memory.

She had danced, one night with Warren in college. Joshua was long gone; out of the picture. And Warren had been there, again. And she remembered telling him: "You drink too much." And he laughed wondrously over the drunken bar music with a familiar sticky floor.

"C'mon, we're in a college bar...don't lecture me." And when he paused to kiss her, she pulled back, slightly, although she had not minded, really. When the music quieted down she told Warren she had to find her roommate and get back to her dorm. It was the easiest and simplest way out.

"See, told you we'd see each other again." Warren had said. It seemed like he forced a smile.

Liza remembered leaving not knowing where to find her roommate. It almost seemed strange, for Liza, that she avoided a kiss and what it might lead too from a young man she had known for four years for a roommate who, as it turned out, was her assigned, dormitory roommate for just one year. Liza got an apartment the following year and lived with someone else whom Liza believed had lesbian tendencies. No other woman touched and hugged Liza more than Deena Kolish and, on the one inevitable occasion, Liza had, eventually, felt uncomfortable around her. And, thinking back, Liza had a difficult time trying to understand exactly how she felt about Deena. They never did stay in touch.

It would not take long for Liza to become surprised at her very own attitude. She became bitter in her developing selfishness manner. And she was immediately aware of this. After all, who does not believe they are taken for granted when the idea of success is hard to come by? This was about the time Liza became aware of her trust and faith in people fading from her fairly rapidly. It was not like a pure paranoia, though. Liza, simply, began to feel like she were entirely on her own and, most of the time, she did not mind so much.

2

Joey Devdenko sat at the foot of his bed. He had never had this feeling before his senior year of High School. And it felt like it would not go away. He was tired but could not sleep. He was spending more time in his room for no particular reason. He was spending most of his time thinking of the future. Joey had not admitted this to anyone but, for the first time, the thought of the future scared him. His prospects and the future crowded him within his own bedroom walls yet he resisted going outside. He was rarely encouraged to leave the house. Joey wished his mom was still alive.

Even the music Joey liked to listen to was not sounding good to him. Turning the volume up did not help. For the first time the loud music he had enjoyed did not disguise the angst or inspire anything creative within Joey. Too often, the songs were violent or sad or about lost love and these things began to make Joey feel worse or—almost worse—nothing at all. It seemed the only time Joey moved from the bed was to lower the volume on his music player. Joey became increasingly tired of the repetitive lyrics: "baby", "love", and the angry young men, older than him, validating their successful points. Sense began to confuse Joey for the first time. He could not play guitar or sing. What was the point of listening?

He eventually turned the music off and spent a good part of that day listening less and trying not to feel nervous. He had not applied to any colleges. He could work at a machine shop. But he did not want to think about that. And, as Joey could not ignore the sounds in his head, his mind began to predictably wander to friends from his school days. They were no longer friends, though. Most were gone from his life. And it, somehow, made him sad to think about them.

They came back to life at a time when 'hanging-out' at the local Youth Center, usually, kept kids out of trouble. He thought it strange how the friends from Elementary School seemed to be all but gone by High School. Joey tried not to think about Ellie.

Joey tried not to believe or feel how fast seven years had gone by since he had been hanging-out with Jackson Blauser. Jackson was big for a sixth-grader. Joey was in fifth-grade at the time. Jackson had had a reputation that matched his size, and despite the one year age difference—which seemed like more back then—they had become inseparable. And Jackson seemed to have no fear. It helped to break the monotony in Joey's early life. Even then Joey was easily bored. And school sucked; living for the summers. And Joey was safe having the older Jackson Blauser as a friend.

When Jackson told Old Lady Swanson to "Shut-the-Fuck-up" because they could get hurt playing with firecrackers or climbing the trees in the neighborhood or smoking a cigarette at such a young age, Joey was the one who stuck-up for Jackson when it seemed every parent in the apartment complex was outraged at such language towards the "Old Bat", as pretty much all the kids called Mrs. Swanson. Jackson's father had actually hit him while his mother stood by with her hand over her mouth. It was shocking to Joey how old and unattractive Jackson's parents had become, and still seemed to Joey on this day. Jackson's parents seemed old and stern and they could not have been much older than thirty. Jackson swore to Joey:

"Those motherfuckers will never hit me again!

"Does your mother hit you too?"

"No. You know what I mean." Jackson had responded while actually smiling at Joey. "I kind of like your mother, though.

"Yeah, she's okay."

"No, I mean I like *your* mother. She's fucking hot!"

"Oh, man, don't go there." And they laughed at the implausibility of Jackson and Joey's mom. "Besides, she don't even know you're alive."

"Ouch...", and Jackson added, "What? No smart ass comment about my mom being black?" He playfully goaded Joey.

"Well, she's okay too..."

And Jackson waited.

"For a darky." And they laughed together.

And Old Lady Swanson did not seem so bad to Joey on this day. Her children had decided it would be better for her in a 'home' for senior citizens. She ended in a hospice. Mrs. Swanson, probably, had not deserved that final treatment.

And Joey thought, briefly, about calling Ellie. But, then again, he was not sure what to say to her. With their senior years upon them their relationship seemed to be strained by an unforeseeable distance. Joey got depressed thinking about her. He had known her since Elementary School and thinking about her had always been easy.

Had Ellie been there that one day at school? The day that one kid...Joey would sometimes forget his name...everybody seemed to like the kid...blonde hair and he had stood-up to Jackson...and it was bothering Joey he could not remember his name, again, and the incident Joey found himself regretting soon after because the kid died in a car crash with his mother about a year later. He never even made it to Junior High School.

"God, what was his name?" Joey wondered, surprised at the sound of his own voice.

Joey could not stop feeling like he was wasting his time; wondering if anyone would care if he were missing...

When Reese Mannion awoke after the operation he knew he was not dreaming. He was extremely tired. He blinked his eyes and it was seconds before he was able to focus. His father was the first person he saw.

"How's mom?"

"She's okay." Reese looked at his father as closely as he could. His dad's eyes were glassy, puffy, and wet. And his dad smiled at his son for thinking of his mother first. "She's wondering about you too."

It was almost next to impossible for Reese to believe that this day had come and gone so fast. His mother had volunteered her kidney immediately when the doctors knew they had a match. She had been adamant.

"That's my son. I still have a good one." And his mother's smile had reassured him. The thought of a transplant had horrified Reese to the point his only release, initially, had been anger. The unfairness was beyond logic. But when his mother had sounded so assured and confident, it was the first time Reese had felt positive in quite some time. Maybe there was a chance to be young and healthy again.

Twelve years later Reese was with his wife driving to his parent's house for a visit. It was not even a holiday. The family was never far apart and a weekly visit was not unusual since they lived in the same city; a friendly suburb in the Midwest; one of thirteen suburbs in the same county surrounding Forest City. But Reese had to admit—and only to himself—this visit seemed a little strange to him. A little uncomfortable for—again he had to admit only to himself—what he knew were selfish reasons: The monotony and responsibility had already begun, and he was only 30 years old. Yet he always seemed to feel he was progressing slower than expected. Reese looked to his left where his wife Kay sat. He had convinced himself she was more enthusiastic about the trip despite the fact they were visiting his parents.

"Feel anything yet."

"You don't have to ask me every ten minutes."

"Oo-kay," Reese looked at her face as she stared straight ahead with her hand on her belly, "didn't realize that was a problem."

"Watch the rode."

"Wow. Who are you? I don't even recognize you right now. Care to terminate."

She turned her head to look at him. "That wasn't very funny."

"I am watching the rode. I can watch the rode and watch you get bigger as we speak. And watch you get pissed-off for no good reason—besides birth.

"Thanks for telling me I look bigger—you ass." She was not to give-in easily.

"You're welcome!" Reese said sarcastically, not watching the rode. Kay sighed and shook her head obviously.

"He's gonna' want out, now, and get the hell out of the car the way you drive."

"Really?"

"Red light."

"I saw it."

"I know." Kay turned quickly and smiled at Reese. Her hair fell in front of her right eye. Kay flipped her dark hair behind her ear. "I was thinking about the job."

"They can't let you go..."

"Well, they left me some doubt."

"...Not because you're pregnant..."

"They almost make it sound like it wasn't part of the contract."

"...Unless you fuck-up the books or something."

"I'm not going to 'fuck-up' the books or something."

"Well, then, you've got nothing to worry about."

"We've got nothing to worry about."

Reese liked to recall moments like these. They sometimes came to him like childish dreams years after the fact. Years of traveling the same road, he sometimes felt, were devised for boredom, and monotony would develop enough variety to keep Reese and Kay on their toes. Having kids will do that, he reasoned.

Warren Teare walked-out of the bank another car lease payment behind him. He was relieved but he really was getting the feeling 'leasing' was not a good idea. He was perpetually a day late with the payments and the bank insisted on charging him the $25 a day late fee in the process; and he was on the verge of paying extra for the mileage he had put on the car. He did not feel like he had driven all that much. It was the first time Warren understood why some people would, seriously, consider robbing a bank; just to get even, so to speak.

It was a nice day, though, and he immediately appreciated being out in the sunshine. He was prepared for the glare and hooked his 'shades' onto his glasses. As he approached his used silver Pisces Warren lit a cigarette. He had liked the car, although it was shaped like a box. It was not pretty on the eyes, but it had run and maneuvered well during the winter months; kind of like a small tank; low to the ground; effective. And, as he reached for the door, he thought he recognized the, somewhat, plain, thin redhead in the passenger's seat of a bright red Pick-Up Truck. Warren watched her. She appeared to be rummaging through the glove compartment with the window down and the engine off. And she glanced at the not soon to be stranger, down and then up again, causing Warren to smile. He knew she would recognize him.

"Warren!"

"Hey Gwen." Warren realized how much easier it used to be to recognize people and acknowledge them. He could not remember how long it had been since he had seen her last. Gwen watched Warren, her eyes focusing, memory rolling.

They would probably never been considered great friends but whenever their paths crossed they talked to each other with general ease. They never challenged each other's weaknesses.

"Did you go to the five year reunion?"

"Hell no," Warren was surprised, after his response, that it had been pretty much that long since they had seen each other, "nobody I wanted to see."

"Same here," Gwen smiled, "too soon anyways...felt like we just graduated, know what I mean?"

"Sure do."

Warren tried to remember why they always seemed to get along. They had not really known each other that well in school. They had met in Junior High. That was actually the time they had gotten along the best, talking and laughing like happy, generally untroubled 14-year-olds. They had not been in any classes together in High School but they still saw each other in the hallways and, on occasion, were the reason they might arrive late for their next class. Warren believed their simple connection was their common nationality. But they hardly ever talked about that. They always found something else to talk about.

"There's someone I want you to meet?" Gwen said from her seat.

"Jesus, do you have a kid?"

"No," Gwen laughed, "not yet." Gwen was looking over Warren's shoulder. It did not take long for Warren to realize her boyfriend or husband was approaching. He looked quite calm and did not appear to have a suspicious or jealous bone in his body. Warren was surprised. And then he looked familiar too.

"I know you." Gwen's friend said. And it hit Warren in a flash as he blinked. Warren had known his wife. And all too well, as it turned-out. It had become quite an ordeal right down to hoping the husband never found out. The guilt and the fear began to slowly seep into Warren's veins. Had he ever found out?

"Randy." Warren said, remembering his name.

"Remember my wife...?

"Yeah," Warren pleaded ignorance, "uh, Meg, right?"

"Right. We got divorced." Randy said, looking at Gwen. She smiled at Randy. Her red hair shined in the sunlight. Randy's hair used to be longer and darker.

"You lived next door to the Kinsman family." Warren was searching for an alibi. "I knew their son Jerry well...we're the same age." Warren felt like he sounded too respectful; almost apologetic. Every word seemed to echo in his head as if the truth wanted to burst from his conscience. The truth was inescapable in his quiet state of panic. Warren concentrated not to talk too much and to leave out as much detail as possible.

"Meg still lives with the kids," Randy added, "...same house."

Warren got the feeling Randy was trying to tell him something; that he was not cheating on Meg, and Warren felt some relief. Randy was not building-up to anything like accusations and infidelity.

"Where do you live?" Gwen asked.

"Apartment by the border...close to the lake."

"Live alone?"

"For as long as I can afford it...how about you two?"

"In town still...on Apex Avenue," she looked at Randy. He had just put his arm around her shoulder, "...just got a house." Randy seemed alright with this.

"Good for you guys."

The conversation ended smoothly. Gwen and Randy were on their way to pick-up Randy's kids at Meg's.

"Take care."

"Good seeing you." And Randy climbed into his red Pick-Up Truck and they were gone again. Warren could not help but think it was appropriate nobody suggested they keep in touch.

Warren quickly decided he had done the correct thing not apologizing to Randy for his one-time, sloppy fuck with his drunken wife.
It could not have done any good, Warren reasoned. Even though the
marriage was on shaky ground—Warren had probably not been the
only one—it could not have been the right time to, suddenly, confess
to something like that. If they had not been drinking the affair, probably, would never have happened. Warren recalled how shit-faced he
was that night, probably more so than Meg. It was surprising to think
how easily she opened herself to him and how she had wanted more
when they saw each other at The Corner Bar that same week. Warren could see that look, the smile, the eagerness for them to go back
to her house because Randy was out of town, again, for some reason
Warren could not remember: Work? Jesus, maybe they had already
broken-up...?! Maybe, he should have gone through with it. But, it was
the kids. Her two kids, three and four-years-old, and Meg was 24 and
basically, Warren concluded, was fucking to retain her youth; trying
to have fun because marriage had turned-out nothing like expected.

Ah, the guilt. He wondered how much she had felt, if any.

Warren—and the thought of 'guilt'—drove away in his used car.
He had been with Meg only once and he supposed he had more than
taken full advantage of an unfortunate situation and had benefited
marginally. As he turned down Apex Ave. driving into the bright,
afternoon sun he thought about stopping at The Corner Bar. He had
not been their since his meeting with Meg two, maybe three years
previously. Warren laughed at this too. And Gwen! What a friendly,
pleasant surprise. Warren had not seen her in almost five years. She
had never looked better. Warren wondered why Gwen had not appeared more attractive to him until they were twenty-three! For the
first time he felt like he might have missed-out on a good thing. But,
then again, Warren never could figure-out how he was supposed to
pick just one.

Hendrik Kuns had loved to listen to his favorite college sports
team on the radio when he was a kid growing up in the east.

"...Wynsander College," the local radio announcer had said at
the time, "has hosted their first tournament championship in their

fourth attempt...The Thanksgiving Invitational is theirs after an up-set victory over New England State...The thirty-five hundred fans that showed-up for this game got a taste of history as the Islanders beat the eastern powerhouse for the first time in twelve tries!" The announcer paused. Henry—as most of his friends and family called him—could hear the student section in the background chanting in victorious celebration of their now proud basketball program. "Wynsander may well be on their way to their first winning season..." Hendrik just could not get enough. He almost felt responsible for their success because it was not until he started paying attention to the school's basketball team that they finally had a season where they did not lose 20 games. They had gone 14-14 the year before and Hendrik believed they were destined for greater success and The National College Basketball Tournament later in the year.

Hendrik planned on attending Wynsander College, a quaint lit-tle school off the east coast, literally on an island to itself where sail-ing, boating, and fencing were major campus activities. There was no football, soccer, or hockey at this school, but Hendrik did not care. He loved basketball and baseball and he loved the island where his parents had taken him on vacation when he was just old enough to appreciate the ocean-side water-park and the tourism. And the idea of the small college and the locals who loved their close knit com-munity and *their* college and the support of *their team* even when they were not winning. It was a real college town on an island where the scholar-athlete progressed and achieved without suspicion.

It was not surprising to see most of the students continuing to reside on the island during the summer when most were not even tak-ing classes! This amazed seven-year-old Hendrik to no end. It made him want to get better grades. And attend Wynsander College.

And then the family moved to the Midwest. Hendrik was crushed.

But, it did not take Hendrik long to realize he could still attend Wynsander when it was time. He just had to maintain his grade point average. And he could still follow the basketball team even though he was a nine hour drive away. Hendrik knew it was nine hours because he made sure to know exactly how long the drive had taken when that fateful day had come and he was in the back seat of their Station Wagon for the entire drive pulling a rental trailer full of furniture.

They had been forced to move back to the Midwest because his parents were actually from there.

"Henry," his dad had told him, "I got a better job...and besides you have aunts and uncles where we're moving to."

This did not sound badly to Hendrik. And, since he was a surprisingly good athlete, even for his smaller size, Hendrik had little trouble making new friends. Hendrik met Warren Teare the summer before the 4th-grade and they were friends almost instantly.

"You really want to go to school there, huh?" Warren asked Hendrik. Warren was actually the only kid who called Hendrik by his real name and Hendrik always appreciated that. Hendrik said to Warren once "I think you like my name better than I do...want it?" And he sort of laughed at his own comment.

"Your name's original...it's kinda' cool. It's cool your parents named you after your mom's maiden name." And Warren paused. "But, no, I don't want it. It's yours." And they would laugh with each other.

And Hendrik would answer Warren more than once, as time went by, about his future school status. "Yeah, I do wanna' go there."

"If you're good enough, get a basketball scholarship. I remember that team they had a couple years ago...wasn't there starting line-up all white?"

"One black guy started...but their first player off the bench was white and he usually played more than the other guy."

"What were their names?"

"Perry Leonard and John Farlow."

"Damn, you were a fan."

"Farlow was a fan favorite 'cuz he transferred from the Southern Military Academy to go there.

"No kidding."

"Yeah. Their point guard was a transfer too. But their best player was actually from the Midwest."

"Yeah, I remember him...what was his name? Van Meyer? He was awesome in the Tournament. Whatever happened to him?"

"He got drafted."

"You do mean basketball, right?"

"Yeah, silly, Professional Basketball...he plays for River City."

"Good." Warren was relieved. "What a waste if the military had gotten a hold of him."

They always agreed on such matters. Wars sucked. Sports were awesome. Black athletes were usually better than white ones, especially in basketball. And discipline did not have to inspire violence. They were young, but these basic beliefs would remain true to them.

As time went by, though, basketball would not be the sport Hendrik would thrive at, although he continued to play two sports all through high school. Baseball was the sport he grew into. After reaching the maximum height of 5'8 Hendrik knew early-on he was too short for basketball. But, with baseball he fit. And, with an almost profound improvement of his hand/eye coordination coupled with a surplus of quickness and speed—he could run the 40 in 4.5—Hendrik's baseball prospects did not appear to be too farfetched.

Liza had decided to move down south after she graduated from high school. She took her first college courses at a State University in the middle of the Sun Belt. Her older sister, Shana, was 22 when she moved south, transferring there two years earlier after attending Junior College for two years. It had been an easy choice for Liza. The first year there, despite some early freshman nervousness, was almost perfect. The ocean was only half-an-hour away.

"I did good on my English test." Liza's hair was bleached from the chlorine in the pool she swam in at least twice a week. Although she was not on the swim team, anymore, she loved to swim at the local health spa. Students received memberships at half price.

Shana was considering how close she was to graduating as Liza glowed over her latest test score. They both had blue eyes and Shana's hair was not as blonde.

"Do you wanna' go to the beach this week?" Shana asked. She looked at Liza who already had a sharp tan accented by her chlorine bleached, sun drenched hair. "It looks like you were there not too long ago."

"Nope," Liza smiled at her sister, "I think you've just been a little busier with school lately...close to graduating." Liza knew her sister was only twelve credit hours away from graduating and one of the classes she could take was physical education.

"Yeah, let's get out of this city for a couple days. I don't have to work at the hotel this weekend...should be a good time to go." Liza loved that her sister had stayed spontaneous while they were in college together. "I've been indoors too much...gotta' work on my tan."

At the beach that weekend, almost a year after graduating from a high school more than six-hundred miles away, Liza experienced the single most, unbelievable 'small world' coincidence of her life. There stood Norman Godette, one of her early boyfriends, with his mouth agape when he realized he was seeing Liza Maine.

"Holyshit!" Norman blurted. He was 6'4 and appeared to be thinner than before. Liza's first thought was how mediocre he looked in his swimsuit, standing on the beach waving at her. He was hairless and without a potbelly, though. "I can't believe it's you!" As he approached Liza could see and remembered the small line of fuzz below his naval. She forced an early smile.

"This is a shocker." Liza said.

It turned-out Norman had remembered Liza was attending college in the area and was actually thinking about trying to find her in the city. Norman laughed while he spoke. Norman and his college roommate had made the three hour trip from their Carolina College with a sophomore from their dorm who had first come to the beach the year before on spring break. Everyone's semester testing was over so they decided to make the trip since the weather was cooperating. Norman continued to laugh. He did not know where the sophomore was at that time (Liza could never remember his name) and they both laughed together when they saw Norm's roommate, Ted, talking and pretty obviously flirting with Liza's sister Shana. His eyes were complimenting her as she lay on a beach towel, smiling a bit herself as she mostly listened to Ted's lines. He stood over her with a paper cup filled with 'sodapop', Norman winked. Ted, feigning unaware, splashed a small stream of his golden, flat, warming libation onto the sand. They all seemed to be laughing. Ted's red plastic cup seemed to be cracking from use and the heat.

"Your buddy a player?"

"He might be." Norm smiled. "Your sister don't seem to mind."

"No. But..." Liza wondered if Shana was just being polite.

It was not long before Shana was seen shaking her head, but smiling, and Ted turned his empty cup upside down, shrugged, and walked towards Liza and Norm.

"Anyone want a cup?"

"Yeah," Norman said, "we should be okay. Be sure and throw the empties in the garbage."

"Yes dad." Ted said facetiously.

It was not long before another car of Norman's friends appeared with at least three more—as Liza remembered—sophomores. Or, it might have been two sophomores and one freshman, but as it turned out they were all in the same fraternity and had been planning the trip for weeks. Norman continued to be amazed by the meeting and began reminding Liza how good she looked.

"You always did like to compliment me, didn't you?" Liza had said.

"You've grown up so..." He gushed, swallowing more beer.

"Oh, stop it you knucklehead." Liza laughed and drank from her plastic cup, but decided she would not offer any of her 'herb' to anyone; only her sister. And that would be much later, unless Shana asked her to partake sooner.

Later, as the day passed and the sun began to set Shana leaned towards her sister as the temperature began to go down. Shana—with exaggerating intent crossing her arms and hunching her shoulders to display the need for warmth—told her sister they should probably go back to the city.

"Should we...before we go...?"

"No." Shana said, whispering. "You brought some...?"

"Of course, let's go."

And after a couple of goodbyes and surprised looks on the faces of the fraternity boys Liza did hug Norman. "Bye," Norman had said

with a right-armed squeeze. His left-hand held a plastic cup not spill-
ing a drop. And the girls left.

They debated whether they were okay to drive the half-an-hour
back to the city after the cups of canned beer they drank. They eyed
a couple of motels but continued towards the city with no worries except the usual moment of directions: Left or Right to get to the highway. They admitted to secretly dumping some of the warm beer in
the sand so no one would see. They did not really drink that much.
"Beach parties used to seem more fun." Shana had said when Liza
asked her if she had had a good time.

"Great. You're getting old." Liza said with a nudge and a smile.

"I was thinking about Bob too."

Liza let Shana talk about the guy she had met at school two
years earlier. They had been inseparable for the first year and, then,
when Bob had stopped calling Shana had surprised her self by con-
tacting Bob, specifically, to see how he had been. Apparently Shana
and Bob were wondering if they were a couple, again, or would be
after graduating. At least Shana was pretty sure Bob was about to
graduate too. That seemed to be part of the problem.

Shana concentrated on the drive back to the city, parking her
purple hatchback in its usual spot on the street not quite a block away
from the duplex she had lived in for just over two years. It was hard to
believe it had been that long already. It was hard to believe Liza had
decided to move in with her. She thought for sure Liza would want to
stay closer to 'home', where she seemed so familiar and comfortable.
She had had so many friends. When Liza had told her she wanted to
move south and live with her and enroll in college, Shana had been
excited and surprised. That was why it was going to make it more
difficult for Shana to tell Liza what she was doing after graduation.

"Roll one would ya'?" Shana asked Liza.

Liza suspected something was on her older sister's mind. Shana
poured two glasses of wine without asking Liza if she wanted any. It
was not the red table wine, either. It was the darker cabernet which
might not have been Liza's choice since the red was sweeter, but she
did not argue. She knew her sister was ready to talk about something
important. Shana had gotten serious about safety and the speed limit

and, then, hardly said a word for about 15 minutes while driving in the car. Liza took her wine, which Shana had poured in one of their two, crystal wine glasses, set it on the brown coffee table next to her papers and finished a tight one. Liza twisted the ends and lit. She inhaled modestly; the paper and the herb joining and burning appropriately, and passed it to Shana. Liza sipped her wine and thought of the sweeter red wine.

"Is everything all right?" Liza asked.

"Yeah, pretty much." Shana had already exhaled. "You do roll those good."

"What's up sis?"

"Did you ever go out with that Norman guy from the beach?" For some reason Shana could not rush into what she intended to tell Liza.

"We went to a movie once...with some other people", Liza was not ready for the interest in her friends from high school, immature or not, "we were in some classes together...always got along. We never slept together if that's what you mean?"

"I could see the way he was looking at you...seemed like he really liked you. Boys do like you."

"I guess that could be part of it...there just boys." Liza started to feel uncomfortable. "Besides, remember Joshua?"

Shana did. "Do you know what happened to him?"

"No. Don't really care." Liza fingered the stem of her wine glass. The wine tasted much better than the beer. "I'm pretty sure he did time for statutory rape."

"I guess I'm surprised you haven't made more friends since you moved here."

"You mean a boyfriend don't you?"

Shana nodded. They both took another hit, softly controlling with their lungs. They held-in and wasted little.

"What did you want to tell me?" Liza asked, sipping her dry wine.

Shana nodded some more and spoke her truth.

"It's almost definite, after I graduate, Bob and I are going to move to the Coastal Keys. Might even take graduate classes down there..." Her voice trailed off because the most important part had already been said. The move was the definitive fact.

"I'm not too surprised." Liza did not look up. "You gotta' do what you gotta' do." Liza felt a little down but she was not upset. She had already realized and learned that people leave. It seemed to be the nature of things. "Mojitaville, eh?"

"Want some more wine?" Shana asked.

"Get the other stuff, would ya', it's sweeter."

"Good idea. It probably will taste better with this."

Liza knew her sister would agree with her. There was absolutely no reason to have a disagreement, especially, over what would be good for their 'high' taste buds.

Before the night was over they talked with their neighbors in the duplex downstairs. The two college students had lived there when Shana first moved-in and she wanted to tell them she was moving too. All four ended-up partying most of the night away and Liza thought it kind of amusing it was the most fun she had had with their downstairs neighbors the entire year Liza had lived there. Shana and one of the neighbors (Liza would have difficulties remembering their names for years afterward) even shed small tears while they sipped and smoked. One of the neighbor girls even went back downstairs and returned with a wonderfully thick tuna-casserole dish for them to eat, which seemed very nice, especially, at the time.

They basically stayed awake, reminiscing about the previous year, until they could not keep their eyes open anymore.

"I heard you through the ceiling, one time." One of the downstairs roommates reminded Shana. "Uh, who was the guy and was he THAT good."

"That must have been Bob." Liza answered for her sister while the roommates tried not to laugh. And then Liza thought she could see a hint of natural blush on her sister's cheeks. "Wasn't it?"

"Nevermind." And the collective laughter did not include Liza. "Give me that wine bottle...I need to put that to use." And they all laughed a little louder, although Liza remained a little stunned and unsure.

They did not sleep until the sun came up.

Joey woke from a short sleep. He was still in his room and it was quiet in the apartment. Jackson Blauser still lived in the same apartment complex across the street with his mom and dad, but Joey could not remember the last time they had seen each other let alone spoke. High school and the one year age difference had separated them somehow. Joey thought about walking across the side street, through the courtyard and buzzing his apartment to see how he was doing. But, he never did. At least not so see Jackson.

Joey began to wonder if Jackson's mother had said something to her son. At this point he was not even sure if Jackson's dad was living with them. Joey had seen Mrs. Blauser a few months earlier...

"Hey Mrs. Blauser," Joey had said. They were both standing in the check-out line at the Discount Store not more than a mile from the apartment complex.

"Joey! Oh, call me Connie. I can't believe it...haven't seen you since..."

"The funeral," Joey quietly finished her sentence for her.

"I'm so sorry about your mother...it was so sudden."

"Hard to believe that was two years ago."

"Oh, that long?" Jackson's mom said.

Joey caught himself staring. She really had not changed much since he had first met her ten years earlier. If anything she was thinner than she used to be.

"You look good." He told her.

"Oh, you're sweet."

"How's Jackson?"

"Graduated...but, you knew that already." She paused. "Okay I guess...working part time, downtown, at the Bus Terminal." She kind of laughed.

"Really...that might be interesting?"

"Yeah, might be."

Joey asked Mrs. Blauser if she wanted help with her bags since she had three bags and he had just one.

"Sure. Thanks." Once the bags were in her trunk Joey said it had been good to see her again and turned to walk away. "Why don't you stop by the apartment? You know where it is."

Joey nodded.

"You can carry some of those bags up the steps for me."

"Okay. See you in a few minutes Mrs. Blauser, after I drop off the milk."

"Okay."

Joey turned towards his car and turned around again to ask something.

"You think Jackson might be around?"

"Uh, he might be."

"Okay Mrs. Blauser, see you in a few."

"Oh, and Joey...?"

Joey stopped to turn again.

"Yes?"

"Call me Connie."

"Okay." Joey smiled and turned for his used car, not remembering for a second or two exactly where he parked.

After Joey dropped off the milk, bread, and mayonnaise, he locked the apartment door, exited the building through the first floor—after being sure it locked automatically—walked across the side street to the other apartment complex, through the courtyard, up two cement steps, passed the separation of two buildings and their backdoor entrances, down two cement steps, and approached the parking lot where Jackson's mother stood next to her car. Discolored and fading red and yellow leaves were strewn all over the parking lot, fallen from the surrounding oak trees that stood about as high as the apartment buildings. The two smaller birch trees, carefully planted in each apartment complex courtyard, within the oval-circle path of the sidewalk—Joey had shortcut through the grass to get to the parking lot—were soon to follow suit; their once bright, autumn colors also fading. It was a sign winter was no more than a month away.

"That was quick." She said as soon as she saw Joey.

"Right next door."

"Thanks again." She said, handing Joey two of the three grocery bags. They proceeded to walk-up the two steps Joey had just descended and entered through the locked door to the right. They walked the four flights of steps that spiraled upward at right angles, a platform at each level.

"Probably the worst thing about living on the fourth floor..."

"Only one elevator at the main entrance," Joey said, "our building's the same way."

Joey watched Mrs. Blauser from behind as she walked down the hallway with her keys in her hand. She unlocked the door and stepped inside. The kitchen was straight ahead passed a narrow hall and a closet. Joey placed the bags on the kitchen counter where she pointed next to the stovetop and the burners, balancing the one top heavy bag, slightly. A loaf of bread tried to roll-out.

"Jackson, are you home!" His mother called-out. She did not have to yell very loud in the reasonably spaced apartment. The dining room and the living room were one square room behind the kitchen wall with two doorways about ten feet apart. There was one 'bay' window that overlooked the parking lot where Mrs. Blauser parked her car. And there was the other hallway that led from the living room, opposite the entrance, where there were two bedrooms and the bathroom. Joey almost smiled, familiar with the similarities.

"How's Mr. Blauser?" Joey finally asked out of what he thought to be politeness.

"He's okay. Don't see him that much...works second shift downtown at S.I.M. Steel...usually when he gets home I'm asleep."

"Oh."

"Are you eighteen?"

"Yes...just turned last month." It was really the first time Joey tried to figure-out her age. He had been stuck with the idea that she was about thirty but, of course, that was some time ago. He had known of her for, at least, ten years and began the quick math in his head. He did not think it would be polite to ask her age.

"You haven't changed." Joey finally said. Mrs. Blauser paused and smiled, looking at Joey.

"You have! You got a girlfriend taking care of you." Her dark skin always came across like a good suntan. And then Joey thought about Ellie. And her pretty face and her jet black hair, just like his except longer.

"Well, sort of." He and Ellie had already begun to talk less once their senior year had begun. "Did you ever meet Ellie?" Joey asked, although he realized almost immediately he did not want to talk about Ellie.

"No. Don't think I know who she is."

"Is Connie short for Constance?" Joey said, changing the subject.

"Why yes! I'm surprised you remember that!"

"Sure I remember that...used to see you guys all the time, especially Jackson. It hasn't been that long. Jackson told me he was basically named after his dad too, Jack, and it was pretty much your idea not to have a junior so you just decided Jack-son would be appropriate since that was how Jackson came about anyway."

"You two were close for a while there, weren't you?" Mrs. Blauser said, answering her own question.

"Constance is a pretty name...easy to remember," Joey added.

"Oh, that's nice of you. Did you know my parents were mixed too?"

"I think Jackson mentioned that."

"Think you could date a black woman?"

"Um, I don't see why not." Joey was only slightly surprised by the question. "I don't believe skin color has anything to do with beauty. People are people, ya' know?"

They were still standing and Mrs. Blauser opened her refrigerator to put her milk away. "Am I allowed to offer you a beer? There's a whole case Jack bought."

"Do you think he'd mind?" Joey was kind of amused she called her husband Jack and not Mr. Blauser. When he was a kid it had always been Mr. and Mrs. Blauser this and Mr. and Mrs. Blauser that even when they were talking to each other around the kids. She paused for a second.

"Don't see why not. It's only one...or two." And she chuckled, cracking open a can for herself. "Here." And she handed a can to Joey.

"Thanks miss...er Connie."

"See. That's not so hard. Have a seat in the living room. Turn on the T.V. Relax. Jackson might call from the Terminal...sounds so serious...might be nice if you get a chance to talk to him..."

"Is he working?"

"Yeah, if he's not here he must be working a second shift too... his schedule changes...hard to keep track of."

"If nothing else you gotta' tell him I stopped by."

"Oh yeah, sure, of course. But, hopefully he'll call. He might be very late too."

This was the first time Joey realized he would not mind if Jackson did not call or if he got a chance to talk to him on that day. He, really, did not care if Mr. Blauser showed up. Joey vividly remembered, again, that day when Mr. Blauser smacked Jackson across the face for swearing and showing disrespect for the elderly, Old Lady Swanson. He had hit him very hard and had hit Jackson on other occasions too. Or so it seemed. Joey had only seen that one smack. Joey was not sure if he had the nerve or even wanted to ask Jackson's mother...Mr. Blauser's wife, if Jackson had been hit often by his father. Joey's mind began to swim a bit, enjoying his alone time with Jackson's mother... Constance. He became somewhat nervous with excitement.

"Do you mind if I grab another beer?" Joey called out. Mrs. Blauser had departed the living room—after turning the T.V on—to change out of her long sleeved blouse. It was a comfortable, early November day and she admitted she had been wearing the blouse for "two days...time to change..." and had gone down the hall to her bedroom.

"Not at all...go ahead!" She called back. "But take it easy!"

She sounded just like a mom, again. That was something his mom would have said, for sure, if she had not...Joey did not want to think about unbelievable or unforeseen fates.

When Mrs. Blauser emerged from her room, and the dark hallway, she was wearing a white tank top blouse with three buttons in front forming a v-neck. The third button hole was filled and, when she bent over, her blouse rose so Joey could see her tattoo stamped on the small of her back just above her blue jeans waste line. The room was lit low and the T.V was on low. They both agreed they did not

care what was on, so Mrs. Blauser returned to the sofa with the remote control in one hand and a beer in the other. She sat down next
to Joey.

Joey felt his heartbeat.

"There's got to be a good rerun on." She stopped changing channels. They were not really watching, Joey thought.

"How old was your mom?" Joey was a little surprised this time
by the sudden question. She sipped her beer and looked at Joey clearly.

"Forty-eight." He whispered.

"She was older than me. I thought so. She always looked good
for her age."

"So do you."

"And what age is that?!" Mrs. Blauser looked directly at Joey
again. She smiled large almost taken aback while seemingly instigating.

"You know what I mean." Joey focused on nothing on the T.V.

"I don't believe I do." Mrs. Blauser crossed her legs and shifted
her shoulders toward Joey. He could feel her staring at him until he
wondered why that should bother him. Joey slowly turned his sights
to her and they stared. She smiled more than he did.

"It's just a compliment." Joey said oddly uncomfortable by the
praise and the closeness; trying to understand.

"Oh, is that all it was?" Mrs. Blauser seemed to be instigating
still.

"Yes...and no."

"Getting mysterious are we?"

"Yeah, I guess so..."

"And what's that supposed to mean?" Mrs. Blauser's smile did
not seem as bright, fading ever-so-slightly.

"Means whatever you want it to mean, I guess." Joey stared at
her. "I'll grab one more beer, if you don't mind." He chugged to the
bottom. Mrs. Blauser's shoulders did not move, squared-up facing
Joey, legs crossed right over left.

"Uh, yeah, go ahead, just one more if you want." And Joey used
Mrs. Blauser's available thigh to push himself off the sofa. Her fin-

gers brushed the back of Joey's hand after a brief squeeze of her thigh. "Get me one too."

When Joey returned from the kitchen he handed Mrs. Blauser the opened beer can and stood over her, nervously wondering how and why this scene had come to fruition and when or if it should end.

"You gonna' sit down." Her position on the sofa had not changed much. She placed her beer can on the coffee table in front of her and leaned back, again, legs still crossed. "Did Jackson ever mention I can't have anymore kids?"

"No." Joey did not sit down. He walked around the coffee table to pick-up the remote control instead of reaching across her folded legs. He felt conflicted. And then rude for handling her remote control without asking.

"Jackson's birth was tricky. I was twenty."

"No wonder you still look so good." Joey said with remote in hand, not changing the channel. Joey could feel her watching his every move.

"It was safer not to have anymore children." Mrs. Blauser said, smiling; watching.

"Health reasons?"

"And financially I didn't need to take the risk...besides," Mrs. Blauser breathed, "not being able to get pregnant has its advantages."

"Do you wish you could've had another kid?"

"No. One was enough. Especially after the..." And Mrs. Blauser seemed to change her mind. Joey placed the remote on the coffee table and walked behind the sofa.

"Here." He said. "Do you mind?" And Joey began rubbing her neck. She tightened for a second. "Relax." And he kissed her cheek without thinking.

"Oh, really now...what was that?"

Joey was surprised by the abruptness. "Huh?"

"What are doing?" She was smiling, broadly, again.

"Did you mind?"

"You think you know what I want...what do you think I want?" Her smile was confusing Joey. She seemed to be breathing heavily and stood from her seat to face Joey, only the sofa between them.

"I don't know what you want?" Joey was barely audible; just standing in his place; waiting for approval. It remained uncomfortably quiet for Joey although Mrs. Blauser smiled for a few seconds. She dropped to her knees on the sofa never averting her eyes from Joey, awaiting something. She finally grabbed her beer from the coffee table, behind her, sipped, and turned to sit down on her sofa again. From behind Joey could see a shake of her head.

"I almost forgot how young eighteen is." She said to no one in particular. And she stared at the T.V, switching channels.

And the phone rang. Joey prayed it was not Mr. Blauser. It was the most uncomfortable he had felt since the first day of swim class in the 10th-grade. But, this was worse. She let the phone ring three times before answering which made Joey even more uneasy. He suddenly had an uncontrollable urge to leave.

"Hey honey." She spoke softly. "Not much. How about you? How late are you working tonight?" It was then Joey motioned to Mrs. Blauser he had better 'go'. "No, your father is working until midnight..." Her index finger motioned towards the phone as Joey shook his head and placed his backwashed beer can on the kitchen counter and headed towards the door to leave. Joey could here Jackson's mother fill-in-the-blanks and the possible half-truths as he exited the apartment.

"...You'll never guess who I saw today at the store..." She said as the door closed behind him. She sounded surprisingly happy. Joey was surprised how poorly he felt; almost sick to his stomach.

Reese did not look at the back of Kay's head. He thrust and finished with a groan, quick and relatively painless. He rolled-off. Kay did not giggle like she used too. In the other room, almost on cue, the newborn cried.

"I'll go see how he's doing." Reese said rolling to a seated position on the bed.

"Yeah, you do that?" Kay said from her back. "I'm tired."

"Wore you out, huh?" Reese laughed.

"Not hardly."

"Okay." Reese said as he pulled on a pant leg. "Was it that bad for you?" Kay did not say anything as she rolled onto her back and glanced at Reese as he was pulling-on his other pant leg. They remained quiet and Reese hurried to his newborn son. The cries were sporadic and Reese began to talk to his son as he approached hoping the sounds of dad would be familiar and safe. The crying, rarely, ever stopped when Reese tried this. It was normally not until 'mommy' or 'daddy' picked up their son that the crying usually stopped. At least it had gone that way with their first son.

"Oh, man, you made a stink!" Reese observed before he picked up his two-month-old son. "No wonder you're crying!" And Reese carried his second son to the changing table that had been set up in the kids' room. Nathan had used the same table.

"Okay, Norris, let's get you changed."

Not much had changed as far as their relationship was concerned. Reese and Kay had hoped a second child would help them to concentrate on their marriage and family, but as they had been warned by family and friends kids just wear the parents down; always tired; taking the kids to the doctor and eventually school and so on. It was amazing to Reese that Nathan, their older son, had gotten an ear infection before he was a year old. The doctor told them they could expect the same with Norris as he approached a year. It would be difficult to avoid. It was in the family. Reese had had ear infections too. He could not help but wonder how their kidneys would mature. Reese prayed, in his way—they did not attend church on Sundays—that the children would not inherit any other health problems.

Reese got done wincing at the earliest stench of his son's bowels. He threw the wet wipes and the diaper into a specialized diaper container separate from the house garbage, sprinkled some good old fashioned powder on Norris and replaced the diaper with a clean one. He was getting better at this. Kay walked in from their bedroom.

"I'm sorry hon'."

"About what?" Reese pretended. He pretty much knew why she was apologizing.

"My attitude...I'm tired and grouchy...finances...we have to be careful."

"I know...I'm sorry too." What he was sorry about Reese was not exactly sure. "Is the sex getting that boring?" Reese wondered if he had noticed some grey hairs on Kay's head.

"It's just...we have two kids."

"We're taking precautions."

"Did you consider what I suggested?"

"Did you?" Reese looked long and hard at Kay. Her hair was getting grey in front; by her temple.

"I don't wanna' tie my tubes just yet..."

"Well..."

"It's easier for you."

"You think so, really." He watched Kay pull a blanket over Norris. The blanket had footballs, baseball bats, and basketball cartoons on it. Nathan was asleep in the next room. It was late for him. He was going to be two-years-old in two months. "Besides a woman's goods don't last as long as men's, normally."

"That's why you should and I should not," Kay said with disbelief in her voice. "Surprised you had to state that probability," she added and walked-out of Norris's room. "That was harsh."

Yeah, but true, Reese thought to himself.

"Hey, do you wanna' order something for dinner?" When he had to repeat the question Reese knew Kay was perturbed, so he called out again. Reese tried to remember Kay's favorite take-out. "Chinese?" He called, again, waiting for an answer. They had a phone hook-up in the kid's room.

"I don't care," she called back. "Get what you want!"

Reese had little trouble believing they had been married for eight years. They had known each other since high school. Once they had hit thirty years of age Reese had begun to wonder if she still felt the same way about him. Reese liked that when he looked at Kay she still looked the same as she had in high school, except for the grey by the temple and, maybe, ten pounds, but she basically looked the same; made him feel pretty much the same; like they were not getting older, really. They were married. But, time was beginning to go by quickly and there seemed to be no getting around that.

"How about some lo mein?" He called.

"Fine...get some soup too!"

Kay always did like egg drop and wonton mixed together.

"Get the mix?" Reese asked to be sure.

"What mix?"

"Wonton and egg drop together." Good thing I asked, Reese thought. "You used to love that."

"I did?"

"Thought you did...we got it last time." The phone number was still on their phone's 'scroll list' from the two weeks before, but Reese did not bother to mention that.

"Gees, how long ago was that?" And Kay added. "Just get it... that's fine."

"You sure...I thought you said you liked that combination?"

"I said just get it that's fine!" She almost yelled. Reese did not say anymore. He shook his head and talked to himself slightly about how 'she said she loved that stuff'. He dialed the phone and ordered the food for delivery.

"You gonna' pick-it-up!?" Kay called after Reese hung-up the phone.

"No."

"That's a waste of money!"

Reese dialed the number, again, laughing and changed his order to a pick-up. "I still got to use gas to get there," Reese called to Kay after hanging-up the cordless phone in its plastic pouch. Kay did not say anything else. She was probably busy shaking her head at him, Reese began to notice and think more and more.

Warren sat at the bar and waited for his brother, Wolfgang, to arrive. They had spoken on the phone for birthdays and major holidays but had not seen each other in person since his older brother had moved out west. Wolfgang had become a fanatical skier and decided he must live closer to the best ski locations in the country. Wolfgang needed mountains not rolling hillsides. He got a job in a law firm and made the move not long after finishing a stint in the military which had helped him pay for college.

This was Wolfgang's first visit back to his hometown since moving west. Warren had just seen him at the hospital where they were to visit their grandmother. When Wolfgang arrived she had, somewhat surprisingly, just passed, and with not much else to say Warren suggested meeting him at The Corner Bar in the old neighborhood where they had grown-up. The name of the bar had not changed in forty years.

In the meantime, Warren had also contacted Hendrik Kuns in the hopes he might also show. Hendrik had said he would show, was sorry to hear about their grandmother, and was looking forward to seeing Warren's brother again. Warren sort of smiled to himself at the thought of Hendrik and his sincerity. He really meant those things. Wolfgang had coached Warren and Hendrik in their first organized baseball league when they were just eight-years-old and Wolfgang had just begun High School. Warren knew Hendrik really wanted to reminisce about those days.

Hendrik arrived through the front doors first next to the flashing Domestic and Imported Beer sign that hung in the front window overlooking the parking lot and Center Street. The window was tinted just well enough so the customers could see out but anyone driving by from the street could not see inside, clearly, except for the beer sign flashing directly against the window. Customers over fifty years of age were aware of a time when the parking lot in front was once just grass and a yard but had been paved over when it became possible for the first owner to add some parking so that customers on a busy Friday or Saturday night would not have to walk the entire length of the side street passing twenty driveways and their respective homes just to reach the bar. The new lot parked ten cars in front of the building and another ten or so behind those cars just as long as someone was not trying to park a trailer or a large utility vehicle or a 4 by 4 into one of the parking spots. There was no diagonal parking.

Warren looked to his right, again, and Hendrik raised his hand in acknowledgment, walked passed an older man in his fifties alongside a woman about the same age, and then to Warren about three barstools away from them. The only other people in the bar were the bartender and a small group of mechanics from Carlson's Garage located on Center Street too. The three mechanics still had their blue work clothes on with their name tags stitched across the upper left side of their buttoned shirts. It was later than Warren had thought. It was after five o'clock. He wondered for the first time if his brother might have gone back to his hotel after the long flight and changed his mind about stopping at the bar.

"Brother's not here yet?" Hendrik asked.

"Nope...Whatcha' drinkin'? I'll buy." Warren already had a twenty on the bar broken down to a ten, a five, and some ones. "Beers are still cheap here."

"Nobody here we know." Hendrik observed. "I haven't been here in a while."

"Me neither. Not since Meg what's her name?"

"I remember you telling me that story. That's got to be five years, at least."

"Sure is." Warren sipped his beer. "Shit going alright?"

"Yeah...I got that job teaching phys. ed. and an assistant coaching baseball at the Junior College.

"No shit?"

"No shit. Hey, read some of your short stories...noticed you got some print in the Forest City Weekly too."

"Ah, that was bullshit, although I did keep that Weekly, have to admit."

"Liked the story about the guy with the constant hard on... *Wasted Erections* it was called?

"You would. The few people I know that read it liked *The Machine Shop Massacre*.

"Really...?"

"Yeah...hard to believe, isn't it?"

"The twin brothers getting killed by cops at a machine shop while playing laser tag on third shift? The build-up was kind of good because you expected the violence to be from the actual machine shop," and Hendrik thought a moment, "and it was an ironic twist with the cops causing the so-called massacre, but, gees, the best one."

"I agree." Warren said about his own work.

"The twins had beaten somebody in a fight the week before and the cops were supposed to be looking for them...?"

"True." Warren was amused by the recap and review.

"Were you supposed to wonder if the cops knew who they were, in the machine shop and, assumed, they had real guns because the twins were going crazy?"

"Yeah, sure, go on."

"Or," Hendrik continued to guess, "were the police just responding to the possibility of some random activity at the machine shop."

"Fate maybe...well, anyways," Warren bemused, "I'm surprised people liked that one the most."

"You made the one reference to the police getting the description of the twins after the beating...?" Hendrik was contemplating. And Warren continued for him. After all, they were Warren's stories.

"Anyways, that was the one story about bar life...all the stories are, pretty much, about people drinking and maturing and aging and how they change for better or worse...but it was also about the twins being good artists who loved to draw and their drawings were very similar in content and style and becoming a violent release...and they tested each other...drawing the same things without initially conversing...and they were sharing the same, violent thoughts. And, remember, they could barely remember beating the guy who walked in front of their car, and pounded on their hood at the crosswalk, and that's why they got out and beat the guy because they had just painted the car themselves. But, they barely remembered kicking the guy in the head, who was drunk off his ass too, and they stopped when they split his lip, and they drove home mad at the world, mad at work, mad at their father who owned the machine shop, thankful they got the chance to beat the guy because they had been jumped and sucker punched once before, themselves, on separate occasions when they hadn't been together. And that was when they had, really, become inseparable, practically connected at the hip—dare I say like Siamese twins. And they drew some more pictures of ways to kill people at the machine shop. And, so, I don't know, they were together this time—the last time—and they were playing a kids game having fun at work, and they'd come from the bar, buzzing a little, and the bullshit violence that had been occurring in the neighborhood completely ex-ploded in their faces...the one brother got shot in the face. He was laughing at the cops, ironically enough. He was having a great time and wasn't even angry...not taking their warnings seriously because their drawings had become therapeutic—not premeditation—like the police believed because they had seen the drawings."

"And the other twin," Hendrik added, "walked towards the cops trying to tell them 'They're toys. Did you shoot my brother?' and he got close enough to one of the cops that he actually swiped at the pistol pointed at him, and a second cop car showed-up and before the one cop could tell the second car not to shoot because the twin was not armed—he was getting ready to use his taser gun on the twin—one of the other cops saw the twin grab the taser gun and he shot the kid twice, killing him too."

"That was reaching." Warren said so softly Hendrik did not hear him over his own voice and the music that was playing from the C.D-jukebox player.

"After all the talk and all the violent drawings the twins never killed anybody. The only piece of machinery that was plugged-in was the drill press and one manually operated drill making 3/8 inch holes for an airplane part," Hendrik surmised for the author, "about the size of a bullet hole?"

"Well, we agree it wasn't the best one." Warren said, swigging from his beer glass. "And what did you think about the father saying they got what they deserved, screwing around on work hours playing laser tag. He had told his kids they would fuck-up working alone at the machine shop because they were always irresponsible and imma-ture. He'd been embarrassed by them and suspected they were be-coming violent. That was why he showed the police the drawings in their bedroom.

"Oh yeah, right," Hendrik remembered, "the dad did find some blood on one of their shoes from when they beat that guy down at the crosswalk. And then the one drawing they magnetized to their refrig-erator...that was sort of twisted, funny...it was kind of like 'how old are these twins?' They sometimes didn't act like they were twenty-one.'" Hendrik called the bartender over. "Hey, did you know Warren got a book of short stories published?"

"Yes, yes. I could hear what you were talking about." The bartender was younger than Warren and Hendrik and they would not know his name for quite some time. It did not appear he had bartended at The Corner Bar for long. He had a mild accent and sun brown skin. "What's the name of the book?"

"Tales of a Sub-Urban Underground."

"Sorta' remind me of rock band." He set down the two imports. "...on me." Warren and Hendrik had heard a rumor or two of a bartender, or two, getting fired because of giving away too many free drinks. They thought about telling him. They did not. Another rumor had the owner, Mr. Templeton, saying one bartender stopped showing up for work and had no idea what ever became of him. Apparently few people did.

"Did I hear right? Did Templeton sell this place?" Hendrik asked.

"Yes, yes...just last year. I'm just filling in till I find something bettah'. I understand this bar had three owner in forty year."

"Two." Warren plotted over his beer.

"Yeah, we knew Templeton pretty well. His son's the owner now."

"Ah, I see." The bartender looked at Warren. "Little surprised Lou—Mr. Templeton—neva' tol' me that. Do you need anotha'?"

"Yes."

"Templeton ran this place with an iron fist. He took nothing from no one and there was hardly ever a problem or a fight in here—that I can remember." Hendrik finished.

"Sounds right," Warren said, not looking-up. The bartender slid over another imported beer. "Thanks."

"I think his dad's name is Larry," Hendrik added.

"Yes, yes," the fill-in bartender said; not really listening closely, Warren thought.

Hendrik drank an import too and gradually the conversation turned to Warren's brother, Wolfgang, their coach on their first baseball team.

"Hard to believe that was twenty years ago."

"Yeah, no shit," Warren applauded with voice inflection. And he looked from his beer glass to Hendrik. "How many teams were in that league again, and...and...can you name them?" It crossed Warren's mind that he had already consumed two beers and a shot before Hendrik arrived and he should probably slow down. He was beginning to almost burp and hiccup at the same time.

"Oh, let's see. We were the Red Leopards. We had the red jerseys with the black numbers."

"Everybody had black numbers," Warren interrupted.

"No, I think a couple of the teams had white numbers because their jerseys were darker like," and Hendrik paused for effect, "black. They didn't have black on black."

"Okay, well, maybe that one team. Who wore the black uniforms?" And Warren smiled because he knew the answer and he was sure Hendrik knew the answer too. The team in black was the team they could not beat the first year.

"Those fucking Bears...there was no way that first year a couple of those kids were not older than ten. They had to be older. Where's your brother? He should be here."

"Remember the one team who did not have their name written on their jerseys?"

"Yes," and Hendrik was laughing at themselves and the thought of the uniform, "the White Lions! They had that picture of the head of that white lion from those older anime cartoons, we used to watch, on the front of their jersey."

"And they had those light-blue colored shirts," Warren added.

"And white numbers too." Hendrik countered. "I remember. No wonder they were the worst team every year. They played as soft as they looked."

"Oh, yeah, they did have white numbers too...made it kind of hard to see with the light-blue jersey. What was the name of the white lion?"

"Shoot, don't remember," Hendrik said, "can't think of it...show never even came back on reruns as far as I know."

Warren stopped to think of the names of the other teams. The bar was beginning to fill-up and it would not be long before Warren would begin to have a difficult time remembering what happened in what order and what timeframe. Warren asked the bartender if he could drink with them if Warren was buying, and then suggested the bartender ask the two young ladies who had recently entered the bar what they were drinking and "get them some drinks on me". Warren remembered everybody being very obliged as he continued reminiscing about the Forest City Baseball League.

"The Divisions were split in two: The City Division and The Heights Division."

"Right...we were in the Heights."

And between the two of them they recalled the Cougars wore an interstate, sign-blue uniform; the Jaguars wore brown; and the Wildcats wore green.

"And in the City Division, the teams were about 90% black."

"And we were 95% white."

"Remember the teams in the City Division?"

"Give me a sec, I'll figure it out." And Hendrik began to name the teams in The City Division and, between the two of them, they recalled the uniform colors: the Grey Eagles were grey, "naturally", they laughed; the Black Hawks were black with red sleeves and "oh, red numbers" they recalled again which helped differentiate them from the Bears wearing all black with white numbers and lettering; the Falcons wore yellow jerseys with black sleeves; The Gold (as it was literally, boldly lettered on the front of their jerseys, almost forming a circle in front, 'The' on top and 'Gold' bending upward from below, left to right) had to have black letters and numbers also; the Maroons were the only other teams beside the White Lions to have white numbers to go with their eponymous name and color; and The Phoenix were proud to wear a sleeveless, mesh, orange jersey that 'breathed' well so they could where yellow or red t-shirts underneath to display more of a 'fiery' Phoenix combination. They also had black hats and black numbers and lettering. Every other team had a hat that matched their main color except the Falcons who did not want to where yellow hats. They wore black hats with their yellow jerseys and black numbers. And, basically, every team wore white baseball pants. It was easier and cheaper that way.

Hendrik and Warren laughed at their own detail and the time to recall these teams whom they played for when they were 8, 9, and 10 years old. And they laughed some more, and ordered more imports, when they remembered the players had pretty much taken a league wide vote and agreed The Phoenix had the best uniforms. The uniforms were louder than the kids, and that is probably why they loved them, and the parents would shake their heads at their children and smile in disbelief.

"The parents were right, no?"

"Those things were loud." And Hendrik tipped the fill-in bartender for giving them two more free beers.

After Hendrik bought another round for the same two, young ladies from earlier—Warren and Hendrik did not bother to ask the bartender if he were sure they were old enough to be in the bar, he did not seem to care either—they waved back almost excitedly, and one blew a kiss in Warren and Hendrik's direction as they giggled and looked at each other and then raised their glasses together to drink. Hendrik raised his glass quickly also and sipped. Warren smiled at the girls and their giddiness.

"Hey you drunks," the voice was loud in Warren's ear, but its owner was a mystery, "...good to see you gentleman are well on your way!" Warren half-turned on his spinning, barstool-chair with the black seat to find the voice. The bar was beginning to fill-up with the steady sound of music and voices as daylight began to dim. Smoke was beginning to filter upward toward the fan and ventilation shaft in the ceiling. Customers were beginning to walk in exclusively through the back door. The parking lot in front had been filled.

"Wolfgang!" Warren could hear Hendrik's voice from the barstool next to him.

"Hey bro'...!" Wolfgang stood before them sporting blue jeans, loafers, dark socks, and a dark colored sport coat over a pullover, long sleeved shirt made of cotton. He had topped-out a couple inches taller than Warren at about 6'1 and he scanned the room slowly before leaning forward and speaking.

"Hendrik, right...?" Their hands were together, two shakes.

"Did you tell him I'd be here?" Hendrik asked.

"No."

"Hasn't been that long...I remember the old Forest City League very well. I even played you at short ahead of my brother!"

"Man, this is awesome, we were just going over the league and remembering the teams and all...and defending our championship...!"

"And we hated those fucking Bears," Wolfgang had them laughing some more, "the cheating bastards!"

"Remember they ruined are undefeated season when we were ten?" Hendrik was eating up the scene and the memory.

"Hell yeah...! Last game of the regular season...I honestly think the league schedule makers did that on purpose because they realized we had a rivalry with them. Our only loss the year before was to them, earlier, in the regular season!"

"Oh yeah, that's right."

"Both years we won the rubber match!"

"In the Championship Game...!" Warren and Hendrik synchronized.

"Hey, your friend need a drink?" The bartender asked.

"Thanks," Warren answered for his brother.

"Import looks good," Wolfgang agreed.

"On me," and the bartender placed the bottle on a beer-labeled, cardboard coaster on top of the bar.

"I'm starting to wonder if he's gay," Warren laughed at himself and the thought of saying it too loud. Warren was not sure if anyone heard him.

"Thanks again," Wolfgang called out as their bartender walked away.

"We've been buying those two cuties over there some drinks," Hendrik said through his buzz, pretty much, for the sake of saying something over their, brief, conversational silence and the elevating music.

"I noticed that almost immediately," Wolfgang said.

"Did you stop at the hotel before coming here?" Warren asked.

"For a minute...but, I decided to go to the other side of town, passed the ball fields and the old neighborhood where some of my old friends lived. I just kept driving around the old places; even the Youth Center looked different!" They were beginning to raise their voices to speak.

"Yeah, it is different, they don't have the Elementary Schools competing against each other anymore...too many schools closed and are now combined. Population has apparently leveled off, in the suburbs!" Hendrik informed, leaning in.

"Guess that's not surprising! But driving around I felt like I was invisible. Like a ghost in my old town!"

"It would feel even stranger if you felt like that in the town you live-in." Warren said.

"You get that feeling?" Hendrik asked, barely hearing.

"Yeah, sort of...I think that's why I finally started writing."

"Like a ghost, huh?" Hendrik said. "...reminds me of one of your stories!"

"Ha! You must mean the one about the poet who wrote 1000 poems and literally dropped off the face of the earth."

"*The End All Be All.*" And Hendrik recited, "'...and his soul was not gone, but left stirring within the friends he had grown with, sad to live forever, never to grow old...'" And then you wrote how people who had never met the poet before talked to this personable young man who they wished they could see again, and they would be talking about their meeting to someone and the brother of the poet began to think and realize maybe the person telling the story had seen the ghost of the dead-poet-brother just by the description and some of the things he'd said—like mentioning a thousand poems."

"The brother engaged in three incidents where he heard someone claiming to have come across his brother—the poet, after he had died—and as time went by he believed, more and more that they had actually seen his brother and it was not a coincidence that he had conveniently come across these other people who met him 'once' and they wished they would have the chance to hear from him again—like his brother was experiencing. The poet-stranger—or ghost, as the brother would come to believe he had become in spirit—soon became a part of his dreams; and then he discovered his parents also had a dream about their son, the poet, that same night. The poet made a few more random impressions—in the real world—and the people who saw him once would never see him again. And the brother and the parents would, eventually, see the poet less and less in their dreams...it did not seem as necessary. The poet's lifeline was complete; he would remain a part of them, inspiring his brother to begin writing and be a poet too." Warren immediately regretted describing his own story, so much. Plus, he had been forced to practically yell to be heard. So, he stopped. If Hendrik wished to discuss the stories, anymore, that was up to Hendrik. Warren would not encourage it. If anybody else mentioned the stories, Warren would suggest they read it themselves. He had said too much about them already. He had promised himself never to discuss his work in public. Especially in a bar! Warren had broken one of his personal, cardinal rules. "Never talk about your own work." He was almost angry with himself.

"Sorry bro'...! Haven't read your stories yet. But, I will. That didn't sound bad though!"

"Ah, probably the booze," Warren said, slapping Hendrik on the back.

"We need! We need! We need...!" The trio, like stooges, requested with Warren leading the charge. "We need another drink! No more short story synopsis...Promise!" It did not appear the fill-in bartender knew what Warren was talking about and may not have cared. But, he brought more drinks anyway.

Wolfgang began to spend more time walking the length of the bar, to the bathroom, and back, talking to the two girls briefly, and back, the cigarette smoke getting thicker in the air that they would, undoubtedly, smell on their clothes the next day. The music continued, less and less recognizable, as the girls stood and moved to the music, well, wiggling, dancing, and Warren began to wonder if they might be smelling the girls on them, the next day, and one of them approached Warren and Hendrik, briefly, saying "hello" and thanking them for the drinks, and the two girls took turns making their way back and forth, to Hendrik and Warren, "saving their seats" as the one girl told them—God they were young, Warren would remember, but so cute; they might not have been twenty-one, but they did not care; the girls surely did not; having a good time, it seemed—and the one girl "what is her name?" Hendrik asked, but Warren could not remember, and the one girl started to lean on Hendrik, and she was starting to feel good to all concerned, and Hendrik was touching her back, lightly stroking with his fingertips, "Hey, you might want to be sure your coat's..." and "It's ok, my girlfriend's watching" and Hendrik and Warren looked at each other as Warren tried to ask the bartender for more beers, and Warren laughed inside because they still could not get a name from them without asking. Again.

"Get their names?" Wolfgang appeared from nowhere, hovering over their barstools.

"No! You don't know either! You seem taller somehow!"

"No," was all Warren remembered Wolfgang saying. Hendrik was not in the chair, anymore, to Warren's right. One of the young girls was there keeping the seat nice and warm. Warren offered another drink. She said she had just ordered a round as Hendrik requested. Warren thought he remembered the fill-in bartender saying he had to go, his "replacement was here" and "it was nice meeting you" and "be careful" and all that and Warren wondered if he would remember much more. Who's the girl to the right? Where's Hendrik? Where's my brother? And where did the bartender's accent go?

"Where's the Wolf!" He said, to nobody listening. Did he make a noise? Ha. He kissed the girl. Warren did not think he wanted to leave just yet, and he told her so with a kiss. Yeah, sure, for now. It was the other girl and they were wearing their coats, still drinking, one sitting one standing, Hendrik hugged the girl, quickly, and they shared the barstool, Hendrik's knee between her legs from behind. Warren removed his hand from his import and nodded clumsily. Yeah, ok. Yeah, sure. His hands were on his knees and his arm went around her waste without thinking. He was slowing down but still awake. She was cute, he thought, she had small features, and, "look she's got blue eyes", giggling, charming and young, he could still make-out the blue eyes despite the dark of the bar and the smoke hovering in the room, rising slowly, disintegrating but never vanishing; hovering like azure above the bar; floating through the neon signs, and visible in reverse through the mirror where everyone could be seen from their different angle and slightly different perspective, but not the smiles and the different blues as much, hovering, so much hovering, the light, the music, the voices, the blue-white cloud; hoping the new bartender was not getting suspicious! Wolfgang coming and going. Oh, two new bartender's! If the new owner's not here, be ok. I.D might not be needed. They stayed. How long, Warren did not know. He tried not to crowd his blue-eyed-doe. Warren could not believe his grandmother had died. Wolfgang ruffled Warren's hair with a playful hand.

"Don't get all serious on us now...I can't believe either, in a way." That was about the last, semi-complete sentence Warren would be a part of for the rest of the night. If anything else was said or heard, clearly, Warren was fortunate to understand and respond.

When Warren woke the next day he was in his own apartment by the border by the lake. He was in his bed above the covers with his jeans and collared, pullover shirt still on. He laughed because he could smell the perfume from the girls. And Hendrik had left two notes telling Warren to call his house when he was awake.

"...Can't very well call when I'm asleep. What the hell happened last night? They were all here." Warren vaguely remembered. And Warren promptly called Hendrik from his phone hook-up on the kitchen counter below the old, wooden cupboards.

"When did you and the girls leave?"

Hendrik quickly began to explain what happened in the last two hours after leaving the bar with Warren suddenly going for a walk to try and "wake-up", and returning to the apartment—where Hendrik and the two girls waited—in ten minutes, and then "going to (his) room and not coming back-out".

"By the way their names were Sarah and Michelle."

"Think we'll see them again."

"Don't know. I had a pretty good time with Sarah. I think that's why Michelle wanted to leave."

"When was this?"

"You'd gone into your room and didn't come out."

"Oh."

"That's alright. They were probably too young."

"They were over eighteen, yes?!"

"Yes."

"Old enough..."

"I think Michelle started to feel uncomfortable...and by her-self."

"Okay, don't rub it in."

"Did we ever say bye to Wolfgang?" Warren smiled from the other side of the phone at Hendrik, one of the few who consistently said Wolfgang's name properly. As kids, growing up, Wolfgang had inevitably and constantly been called 'the Wolf man' by just about anyone who talked to him or about him.

"Shit, if you don't know, I don't know. I recall he left before we did...said something." And Warren started to remember how Michelle looked. She was long and athletic but not thin. She appeared to have strong legs and a new, short haircut—somewhat longer and thicker in front, covering her forehead—that came to a point at the length and base of her neck. She was blonde and had blue eyes also and, it appeared, somehow had been neglected by Warren and Hendrik.

"When you didn't come out of your room cute, little Sarah sat next to me on the couch and started talking. I'd popped-in a 70's, jazz-fusion C.D and I was surprised she liked it. She was surprised she liked it. At some point Michelle went into your room to see if you were awake or okay. They didn't stay much later than the length of your C.D. What'd you do to her?"

"I was asleep. I think I dreamed someone was standing over me, kind of crowding me. Maybe that was Michelle trying to wake-me-up for a minute, with nothing better to do since you and Sarah suddenly hit-it-off."

"That was kind of strange...Michelle and I were together at the bar and Sarah was amused and hanging around you. She's a little play-er. When we were alone she would get frisky."

"Huh. I don't think I want to hear anymore." And their muddled laughs crossed through the phone lines.

"No menage trois?"

"Nope...Michelle wanted no part of it."

"Hey, did we see Darius Bridgeport last night?"

"Uh, no. We talked about him being one of the best baseball players we ever played against from The Phoenix right-on-up..."

"And what about Freddie Fox?"

"He was one of the few black kids in our Division. Uh, no, didn't see him either. Wasn't he on the White Lions...?"

"Damn. Was I dreaming again?" Warren said, hunting for stories.

3

Joey felt hollow and empty the following winter. He was not speaking to his father much. The holidays were a very brief reprieve, but not having his mother around, especially that time of year, continued to leave pall over the festivities they previously enjoyed. And now that March was upon them the Midwestern skies were another pale shroud of what they could suggest. Autumn, at least, had been colorful. But, now there was rain. And the winter had been cold and long with a foot of snow falling on two separate occasions, once in January and once in February. The New Year had not started well. And March was grey and not showing signs of ending until May. They needed a break. There was little sunlight.

Joey got a call from Ellie one night. They had not even seen each other over the holidays. They never saw each other in school anymore. She almost did not seem real to him and she lived only four miles away. She was a voice over the phone; barely a picture in his head, the jet black hair and the deep brown eyes. He mostly listened as she tried to speak to him. There was cold space and air between them; dead air, it seemed to Joey; too quiet. Ellie asked, more than once, if he was okay. All he could say was yes. He was never sure if she could tell he was lying to her; lying to her about not saying what he thought. He could not say what he thought, especially when she asked him. It seemed Joey would freeze and forget, not knowing what to say. He was losing, failing; succumbing to the pressure to impress without effort.

When Joey had finally left his room to walk during a light rain he did not walk far. But he walked far enough to see Jackson Blauser driving by in his car. He may have been going to work. But Joey did not know for sure. He never did know anymore. Even when Jackson had stopped his car on the side street, by the stop sign to acknowledge Joey, Joey did not speak for long. Jackson rolled down the window and called-out something about seeing Jackson's mom. It had been months ago. Joey pretended he could not remember the details about his visit and Jackson's mother. All Joey heard was how long did he stay and how many beers? Joey just shrugged, unable to face him, unable to acknowledge, wondering why he was unsure what to say in defense of himself; always in defense; why in defense? He turned briefly to wave a hand and jogged in the opposite direction of the stop sign. When he knew Jackson had turned onto Apex Avenue, headed for wherever, Joey returned to the apartment complex; the courtyard; the apartment building; the elevator, not caring if it stopped; the quiet hallway; a stale smell of old carpeting; his room. Joey had taken an old, rock-band poster from his wall as well as two bikini clad models posing, wet, on a tropical beach. They were gone. He dropped onto his bed, aching. It was not the rain. It was not that cold. He thought grey and cloudy like the weather outside. He wished he had talked to Ellie when she asked him the question. They had been friends a long time. She knew about the female babysitter when Joey was seven. He did not talk about that, anymore; the early, sexual experience when he was too young to perform, more than once. Three times, he thought he remembered. He had been so young. There was nobody to blame. The babysitter...? Maybe. Joey did not know whatever became of her. It was like she never existed. Why could he not have done more to prevent it? Why could he not talk about his mother? Why was there a quiet wall between him and his dad? These were all questions they would ask. Ellie, Jackson, Mrs. Blauser, but they knew too much already. He could not face running nowhere. Which way to turn? No place to go; the dead, tired air. Joey was tired; tired of thinking to and of himself

Joey had left the container in his drawer by the bed. He did not want to leave a mess for his father. He had been through too much already. It was not his fault either; nobody's fault, really. It would just be...easier this way. No note. Hopefully, they might think it was an accident. No reason for anger, anymore. It did not matter what was fair, fate, or faith. Joey hoped nobody would be sad, as that last jolt of fear...fear of nothing warmed over him; thinking of a famous British playwright, of all things. Everyone had read him, in school. Some have said the famous playwright was not who he was believed to be. He may have been somebody else; a compilation of English writers. Fake. Joey almost smiled. It was his March. He would do this, himself, with the help or vengeance of no one. It was his March. His own personal Ides...

And Joey dreamed he could not remember or feel.

Warren got a phone call from Hendrik, three days after his grandmother had passed. Hendrik sounded excited; almost worried.

"Are you watching the news?"

"No." Warren did not change the channel in time. Warren had been watching a modern-day, classic film noir and Warren had been surprised he could not think of the name of the screenwriter. Warren was on the verge of explaining this to Hendrik when Hendrik stopped him.

"Man, never mind that. That bartender from The Corner Bar disappeared!"

"What? What was his name?"

"Oh, man, still forget it! But, he disappeared! Didn't show-up for work the next day! The Local News on Channel 4 just showed a picture of the kid from the Caribbean...did we realize that? But, Channel 4 was at The Corner Bar. This doesn't happen around here."

"We don't get many missing people around here?" Warren said.

"Not really. There have been some shootings on the streets in Forest City, but not The Heights...not since that wife's doctor was killed in her home and the husband was accused!"

"Oh, yeah, that was big news. Nationwide." Warren agreed. "But, she didn't disappear. She was found dead immediately."

"No, but, this is big news. Channel 6 had a story on it too! They think he never made it home from the bar the night before. His aunt—who he'd been staying with—did not recall seeing him Friday night."

"Foul play suspected?" Warren asked.

"They're not saying."

"The police must be wondering if he went back to the Caribbean."

"Yeah, but he left everything behind if he did." Hendrik repeated the news.

Warren had missed the broadcast and immediately changed the channel back to the classic movie. The plot revolved around an entrepreneur owning land just outside of Oriental City. He planned on owning the Water Co., and had devised a plan to stop the flow of water—in the desert land he owned—buy the Water Co., and then own and charge what he needed to control Bay City West and Oriental City and the rest of Weston County. The gumshoe, fedora wearing detective was the star of the movie and, slowly, began to figure-out how devious this wealthy man, Rex Barren, had become. Warren was a little surprised there were practically no Orientals in the movie, at least very few with speaking roles. They were simply background in their very own city.

"Yeah, I've seen it." Hendrik had said. "Surprised you're not more interested in the missing bartender."

"I am. I'm interested in both, a little. It's not like I can do anything about either one though."

"Whadya' mean?"

"One's a movie and I'm not a cop."

"Yeah, but the bartender is real...to us."

"Real huh," Warren said. "I guess he is...or was." Warren was forced to differentiate between reality and a detective or mystery story. It was not difficult. He pinched himself and told Hendrik he did so, just for good measure. "I guess that explains the great tan that kid had...inbred from the islands?"

"Yeah, I guess." And Hendrik made an excuse, saying he had to clean and straighten some things in his new house and hung-up the phone. Warren wondered if this might be a good time to begin smoking, again. He had an unopened pack lying around—promising never to break the seal—a sign of the day he had quit years ago. Warren opened the pack and lit a cigarette by the stove-top flame. He inhaled. The flame hummed. He clicked-off the stove. Warren wondered if Hendrik wondered if Warren was hiding something. After all, Warren had to admit, a good or bad portion of that Friday night at the bar, he could not remember. Warren promised himself he would have to call Hendrik back, soon, to see if he wanted to stop at The Corner Bar. Open or not, they might have to investigate his memory, if nothing else.

After throwing out his pack of cigarettes, Warren sat down on the lone piece of sofa in Hendrik's ranch-style house. The house smelled of new carpeting but was barren of almost any style or furniture. Hendrik had one picture on one wall in the living room. It was a black-and-white sketch of Forest City's downtown shoreline as viewed from the Great Lake. There were a handful of randomly placed yellow lights in, or near, the tops of the taller downtown buildings. It was supposed to be nighttime.

Hendrik returned from the kitchen with his bottle of beer and a fold-out chair. Hendrik had a basic cable system hooked-up and they watched a sports channel.

"Are you surprised they closed The Corner Bar...for now?"

"Not at all," Warren said. And, then, Warren did not want to talk about The Corner Bar, after all. Something inside him said to avoid that conversation. He was not quite sure what or why this was, but that is what he convinced himself he should do. "Do you ever think about our two years at Midwest Central?"

"Well, almost two years." Hendrik sort of smiled.

"Did I ever apologize for getting us thrown out of there?"

"I think it was understood. I know it wasn't intentional." Hendrik reasoned. "It wasn't like you planned to get us tossed. They used us as an example anyways."

"The worse part was, your grades were good and they wouldn't give you a break."

"Believe me, I remember. That was about the time you got into a shouting match with the school's representative at that quote, 'Hearing'...he kept cutting-you-down...accused you of setting the fire on purpose because you had been put on Academic Probation for the second time and couldn't play baseball anymore.

"Well, at least you still finished school."

"Forest State helped me get the job at the Community College."

Warren began to relive some of his college days at MC State. Warren had decided to tryout for the basketball team, and they had both been, somewhat, surprised when Warren made the team.

"Hey, did you ever regret not going to Wynsander College?" Warren remembered to ask, pausing from his recollection of Midwest Central.

"Not really. Just a little too far away, I guess."

And the following year—after Warren's grades improved—he decided to tryout for the baseball team and made the squad, again, as a third baseman and relief pitcher. But, again, his grades fell and he was placed on Academic Probation and he was unceremoniously dropped from his second sports program in two years; and then the fire in their underclassmen dorm. Warren had begun burning his test papers that were below passing and a fair pile of burning, smoking ash began to form in Warren and Hendrik's one-room, one-windowed dorm with a bunk bed.

"No, of course it wasn't smart," Warren had said over and over to whomever would ask or listen, "but the fire had been out for ten, fifteen minutes before the dorms Student-Counselors noticed the smoke and called the police on us."

"And remember the freshman in the other wing had torn down their hallway ceiling?" Hendrik had added in their defense, more than once himself. "They were getting tired of the damage being done to the dorm and made an example out of us. Our tile floor got burnt some, and they bitched about the smell of smoke for two days. We did have our own window open all week and it was still cold outside. It must have been April."

Warren remembered walking passed the girls dorm just days after seeing Liza Maine at The Campii Moon Bar and did recall feeling a bit stressed about his grades and being 'cut' by the baseball team and the semi-cold reaction he had received from Liza, now that they were getting closer to life in the 'real world'. Warren wondered if, somehow, Liza sensed something was wrong or something was soon to be wrong. It did appear that some women have a logical, practical defense system that allows them the sense to avoid impracticalities—

even if it negates them of fun. They become distinctly aware of what is beneficial for them—or at least safe—for extended periods of time.

But, it was during this walk that Warren—carrying a case of beer like a piece of luggage from a store about a two-minute drive from their dorm—saw Linda Hodson looking out her dorm window. The window was at ground level and, as she recognized Warren approaching, opened the window without saying a word. She motioned for Warren to approach. She had noticed the case of beer also.

"Hey Linda." Warren said.

"Trade you for some of what I got." Her face was beaming and her eyes were bloodshot. "My roommate's not here either."

"What, she's not partying with you?"

"Hell no...!" Linda said, rolling her big, bloodshot eyes in her head. She had sandy, blonde hair and, as Warren handed her the case, he could finally see Linda below the waste. She was wearing fading, pink underwear with tiny, blue dots that might have been tiny flowers at one time. She was alabaster-white and the pink underwear was snug high to her upper thigh visibly full, white and smooth. The underwear covered her from behind, complete and snug, rounding into shape. She had turned with the case of beer, and her arms shone off the desk light, almost shining through her white, tank-top t-shirt. It seemed worn from many nights of sleep.

"Think you might want to go to our room, later? Hendrik's waiting," Warren said, climbing through the window, feet dropping to the floor.

"He can wait, can't he? I don't want to change just yet," Linda had said. "Besides, I want to enjoy my room with someone besides my roommate. She should be gone quite awhile. She had a full class schedule today. Thank God. She actually gets upset with me if I walk around the room in my underwear."

"That's hard to believe. But, it's probably because she's heavier than you."

"You don't mind, do you?" Her smile was so constant and full it made Warren laugh even more at the question.

"Uh, no..."

"I didn't think so. Here have some." And with bloodshot, smiling eyes and lavender-lips in tact, she handed Warren the half-burnt joint and the lighter. Warren lit-up without saying a word. Linda opened a beer and handed it to Warren as he exhaled. "May I?" She asked.

"Of course, that was the point."

It was a perfect memory for Warren. It seemed the conclusion of their meeting by the window had been pre-ordained. It was one of the few times there had been no innuendos, prolonged teasing, or non-stop foreplay. Linda sat on her desk chair for a few minutes, facing Warren. She told him to take a seat on the bottom bunk, and he did. She stood to hand the joint back to Warren and he felt it almost immediately; in his head; the gaps were closing, filling the insides. The blood was flowing.

"Remember when I saw you coming out of the shower, that one day, when we'd first moved into the dorm."

"Sure do." They had joked about how cold the water was, that day, and it "showed". "What were you girls doing, wandering around the boys' dorm?"

"You don't look cold today." Her smile was becoming and contagious. Linda's mid-drift was at mouth level and her tank-top rose some from her waste revealing her milky flesh, two-inches below her belly-button. Her leg bumped Warren. Her cleavage beckoned about an inch apart. She never looked more complete. Warren spotted the close-up freckles in her cleavage.

"Do you want to?" She asked. Warren had handed her the joint and she took it to her mouth, rubbing her other hand slowly on the top of Warren's head. Warren fingered her thigh and blew a slow, prolonged breath on her freckles and they laughed at each other as her other hand caressed Warren's hair, as what was visibly left of the joint hung from her lip. "I'm so glad you stopped by." And the joint was quickly discarded, falling from the heavily used ashtray, onto the desk, and the alabaster-shapely Linda sat down next to Warren and kissed him, trading tongues, and they tried to position each other and she hit her head on the rail of the top bunk. They laughed and nodded at each other and Linda hopped-up to the top bunk and

Warren helped with a squeeze and push from behind and followed throwing his legs upward with some lift with his hands on the silver rail, bounding onto the top bunk with a lunge and smothered Linda, his hands pushing upward on her tank-top, Linda breathing into his ear—when they weren't tonguing—already appreciating the ceiling space, and she said those words in his ear as she breathed and they laughed at each other, looking at each other, the desk light nowhere near their eyes but creating a shadow at the head of the bed, by the window, over the dark curtains—she had closed them and he had barely noticed—and their body movements rolled on the wall behind her, in front of him, they were causing the walls to move and shadow, and the bed hit the wall next to them and it shimmied, and her hands, from below, had him clear, button-off, zipper-down, and Warren arched back as she pulled downward, from below, and his shoes fell to the floor, and her hands clenched at the small of his back, and she repeated the words she wanted him to do and Warren remembered a deep breath and he relaxed and he rose to his knees and slid her waste toward him, and lifted, and tongued some more and her hands came up behind her and pulled herself back onto her hands, twisting her body a bit, and he was down again as they did their best to use the entire length of the bunk, and she rolled Warren over, onto his back, and she straddled and had the ceiling to work with and "No, no, nobody's cold now..!" And she tried to keep her voice down, laughing, and Warren clutched her waste and used his arms and she finally told him not to, she'd move, she'd move, she'd move, and her hands came down onto the bed, on each side of Warren, and her torso was rocking to and fro with her hips, making the bunk creak of human sounds, together, their bodies, and their guttural throes, rising, and a laugh, a mouth open, teeth clenching, volume condensing, vaguely in unison, and she circled with her torso, longer and longer, and Warren did not have to think, steady, as she circled, and circled, and Warren could vaguely see from the light and the dark and their moving shadow, she smiled at the ceiling, as her hands came off the bed from each side of Warren, and she dropped down to her hands again, quickly, Warren twitched without bending, and she kissed Warren on the lips, as she slowly continued her circumnavigation, he could hear her hands squeeze the sheets, next to his ears, and he squeezed her waste and moved to sit-up, but one of her hands pushed his chest down, and she paused, arms spread, hands gripping sheets, face-to-face, she swirled and circled and Linda was in complete control. She had it right. Warren relaxed. He would last longer if he did not touch her anymore. It was close to perfect—for Warren—as she moved her hips and torso to and fro, back and forth. And her arms began to shorten onto the bed as their faces were closer and her hair fell over her face, tickling his nose; her chin rose from her chest and she threw her hair back with a toss of her head, her eyes opening, smiling. Warren tried to relax, just moving up and forward, slightly, to stay connected. Her body was down on his. Warren felt her bare stomach climbing his torso, toward the patch of hair on his chest, and down and up; her tank-top had never come off. Warren tried to nip at Linda over her shirt and play with his mouth, over her shirt, and he could extend and control no more. His head dropped back onto the bed. His hands gripped her bare waste. She circled, a little faster. The inside of her warm thighs squeezed.

"You'd better get off," Warren did not wish to say, ever, and with a groan. Her bloodshot eyes smiled through the desk light, and their shadow became smaller on the wall behind Warren, by the dark curtains, as she slid her torso forward, and lifted a leg, her half-covered breast rubbing against his lips. "Jesus!" He twitched; motionless. Linda rolled to her right with her back against the wall and did not appear to watch. "That was close."

"We're alright." Linda kissed Warren on the cheek. The kiss, somehow, seemed anti-climactic. Linda got on her knees and bounced down off the top bunk first.

"Think I need a minute here."

"Here." And Linda handed Warren a dry wash cloth. "That's my roommates bunk." And they laughed.

Warren figured he was done—with Linda, at least—for the night and he soon exited the girl's dorm through the same window he had entered, telling her he really should get back to Hendrik because he probably would be wondering what took so long to get a case of beer. Warren left Linda another beer—which she sarcastically thanked him for—and, carrying what was left of his case, Warren walked the remaining fifty-yards, or so, to the boys dorm.

"I remember," Hendrik had laughed, "it took you an hour to pick-up some beer that was no more than half-a-mile away."

"Did you know I tried to stay in contact with Linda, after we got kicked out...actually wrote her once. She told me I was an idiot for playing with fire when I could have just stopped by to play with her—again. That was a crazy, fucking week."

"No, you never did tell me you wrote her."

"She never responded to my letter. She never gave me her phone number, either. I should have realized then, when I said I'd try to contact her over the summer or sometime...she never gave me a number I could call."

"Where was she from?"

"Other side of P.A. Some Ville or Burg...can't remember."

"She didn't get much sun but she still looked healthy," Hendrik had agreed.

"I guess she knew too."

"Knew what?"

"Knew what was good for her in the long-run."

Hendrik sat on his one piece of sofa in the living room watching a horror movie on his digital-video-disc player. It was terrible and he could not believe he had rented it. But, the house was his so he did not mind as much as he might have before owning the house. Plus, he had just installed the movie-player and was glad it worked on the first attempt.

He had had an easy day at North County-Community College. It was not baseball season, yet, so he went straight home after classes. He had already gotten used to most of the students complaining why they had to take Phys. Ed. in college. But, for the most part, the students caused no troubles. The jocks were the only ones who seemed to appreciate the sweat and the physical activity. They, generally, wished they could take more Phys. Ed. classes thinking it would improve their grade-point-averages. Jocks never flunked gym class.

But, Hendrik had become surprised at himself. The last time he had truly enjoyed baseball was when he, finally, became the starting 2nd-baseman for the Forest State University baseball team his senior year. He had tried to walk-on at Midwest Central but had not made the final cut. And, after the suspension from MCS, he enrolled at Forest State and tried to walk-on again. Hendrik, again, did not make the final cut and, by the time he was a junior almost relinquished the idea of playing college baseball. The manager then told him he could receive another year of eligibility if he made the team—even though he had begun his senior year of classes—since he had not played an inning or worn the uniform for a single pitch. The sound of it almost mocked Hendrik, but he convinced himself to tryout one more time.

Hendrik proceeded to make the team and, although he played sparingly, and was close to completing his required classes, Hendrik was ready to make an impression with the experience of being a twenty-three year-old senior the next season. It was the first time in school Hendrik had been considered 'old for his age'. Most seniors were twenty-two, by four years of schooling and graduating standards. But, Hendrik had always been 'young for his age', as most people misinterpreted or phrased it. When most kids turned five during their kindergarten school year, Hendrik had not turned five until the end of June. His parents had managed to get him into school earlier than most. So, after completing college in six years after graduating from high school, Hendrik had become the old, twenty-three year-old senior and no longer the kid who had always been young for his grade.

Hendrik responded by starting every game—with a minor concession. He did have to play 2nd-base for the first time in his baseball life. Every team he had played on, growing-up, he had been the shortstop. But, at barely 5'8 and 150 pounds, Hendrik resigned himself to the idea a bigger shortstop with a stronger throwing arm was better suited to play shortstop at the college level. The game had changed. Their shortstop was, also, their three-hitter and probably the best all-around athlete on the team. And he had been the starter the year before. Hendrik responded by playing with a quick and steady flair while remaining consistent defensively. He made fewer errors than anyone else in the starting infield and, as the season progressed, Hendrik would eventually move from the ninth-spot in the batting order to lead-off. He did that by, steadily, improving his on base percentage and keeping his batting average in the respectable .280 range. He walked almost twice as much as he struck-out, stole 17 bases in 58 games, and scored 40 runs for a team that lost twice as many games as they won. And he had managed to hit one, fence clearing homerun down the left field foul line, just clearing the six-foot high fence over the 320 foot sign! Hendrik, personally, had enjoyed the five triples he managed to leg-out over the glory of clearing the homerun fence. Most of the other 'Jacks on the Forest State baseball team had referred to Hendrik as 'old school' because of his style of play. When the season ended, the eight-team Mid-Northwestern Conference—Forest State finished fifth—awarded Hendrik Kuns the Most Improved Player of the MNC. Hendrik had the plaque hanging on the wall in his bedroom. And, although it had not seemed as important to him compared to Hendrik winning three MVP awards for three different teams growing-up—one when he was 10 (with the Red Leopards); another at 12; and another at 14—he was quietly more proud of the Most Improved Player award. It seemed more aesthetically pleasing to him, somehow. He had worked harder for the college baseball award and, certainly, had not given-up. He enjoyed the awards more than his job at the Community College and working part-time (it felt like) as an Assistant Baseball Coach. The jobs were not as fulfilling. He tried to convince himself it was like being paid a few hundred dollars for summer vacation. But, all that seemed to do was give summer vacation a rather unneeded, duly noted, dull connotation. And, of course, payday always helped. He could payoff the ranch-style house in twenty years, with some luck.

Liza took a last stroll down the one-way streets of her urban, Sun Belt college campus. She walked-up the street where her sister, Shana, had worked since moving to the city. There were not many trees around the shabbily paved streets, the sidewalks, or amongst the buildings. There were two large, circular-stone pots with a small tree in each planted in front of the Marquee Hotel, where Shana had worked the front desk. More times than not the weather agreed and Shana walked from their duplex home to work three or four days a week. There was an outside chance Liza would have worked their soon, but that had fallen through since Shana was graduated and preparing to move farther south with Bob. Apparently he had graduated on time too.

Traffic was thickening on University Street where rows and rows of duplex homes were aligned, almost exclusively, these days, in use for the college students who were attending school there. There were some who had graduated and had not moved and, still others who were living there in pursuit of their continuing youth, partying, and working some, by a college campus. Those students—or ex-students—did not remain long. And there was the occasional small family who lived on that stretch of University Street who tried to live amongst the students for cheap because they could not afford much else; the occasional single parent just hoping to secure a job on the strip so that there children might not starve. But, that was less common than the students or ex-students who refused to leave after graduating or who never graduated but still wanted to stay because they were continuing to have a good time, sharing the house with two, three, sometimes, four people to securely pay the cheap rent. And the cheap rent showed. The duplex homes, really, had not been worked-on or sided or painted in years. As Liza turned onto University St., sometimes, the easiest way to tell the duplex homes apart were the black shuttered windows that were worn and peeled displaying more white than some of the other black shutters; or the screens on the front doors at the tops of four wide steps on large, front porches would be torn or hanging or maybe with a clean tear or hole in the center of the screen door. Some of the wooden, front doors had knockers; others had been taken off. Some of the doorbells that used to work could be seen hanging by their inch-long wires; stiff and dangling by that thread next to the door handle. The driveways were narrow and deceptively long so that two or three cars could be parked behind each duplex where the driveways became small parking lots instead of backyards. It was extremely rare for there to be a garage of any car quantity since it snowed even less than the number of duplex homes that had a garage.

Liza was about three blocks away from her duplex, trying to convince herself she was not going to miss the neighborhood. But, if she was going back to school she decided she may as well continue college in a, somewhat, familiar area. Midwest Central State was only about an hour from where she grew-up and, she was sure this was a good thing at the time, confident she would run into some people she knew from high school. Although, she wondered even then, why that seemed marginally like a pro and not a con. She, still, wanted to believe not being a stranger should be a positive. And Sun Belt-City College and University St. had remained fairly foreign to her. The visit had been, mostly, about taking some college courses and spending as much time with her older sister, Shana. But, that was over.

"Maybe, once we're settled, you could come back down," Shana had told her younger sister. "You could stay with us..." And Shana's voice even trailed-off, unconvincingly, at the thought of it; second-guessing the possible scenarios of marriage, employment, and personal space; all in the blink of an eye.

It had not sounded practical or sensible to Liza either. The situation just reeked of too many what-ifs and she never really knew Bob that well. He did not even have a last name, to Liza, at the time. He was just this Bob character she had only seen a few times and never really talked too. Liza felt she had to try college on her own, in a sense, but not in a city she had barely become accustomed for one year of her life.

When Liza got back to the duplex she borrowed the keys to the purple hatchback and told Shana she was going to checkout the Historic District on the other side of the city. She wanted to see the museum for the last time. The Historic District had been restored by city officials, tax dollars, and the City College alumni. Approximately a three block section of the city had been revived and replicated to appear, pretty much the same, as it had 150 years earlier. There were red-brick roads, and cobblestone roads, and the Olde Stone Church people paid admission to see inside. For an extravagant fee, and plenty of notice, couples could rent the Olde Stone Church for their wedding. Rumor had it the wait, despite the cost, was two years. Liza had planned to park her hatchback and visit the Olde Church too.

But, like so many things that can change in a heartbeat, or—dependent of importance—on a whim, Liza never got to walk passed the Stone Church for the last time. It was too crowded. People and cars were everywhere making it impossible to get within a mile of the Church to walk. It was not that important to Liza to walk almost a mile just to see the Church from the outside. She would not pay, again, to see it from the inside, anyways. Once had been enough to pay. The museum, too, was relegated to a drive-by.

So, she drove around The Square, slowly, in the traffic, forced to stop at crosswalks and traffic lights and got a long glimpse of the Olde Church from The Square and saw a horse drawn carriage mingling with the traffic in the process. The two horses seemed calm enough amongst the crowd of people pointing and the occasional car engine or muffler rumbling, making the air warmer. Liza had her window down and played with the air-conditioning unit, although she knew it was not working. The air came out lukewarm and did not cool.

It was difficult to believe summer was, basically, upon them. It was the first time Liza did not have that excitement about summer approaching. It was 75 degrees and, soon, Liza would be heading north, again, for the Midwest. It did not feel like summer, although it was hot and becoming humid; only a preparation for changing schools. She had three months to kill. And the more she drove the museum disappeared, completely, behind the parade of alleyways and buildings. She was out of traffic and speeding in the other direction.

Reese had not thought about his senior year of baseball in quite some time. Not after Nathan and Norris had been born, at least. Reese had gone to an all-boys school that excelled in athletics. It was a Catholic High School and, although times had changed since the earliest years of the school's existence when all the teachers were priests and there were no women teachers, there had been some women teachers when Reese attended with half of the male teachers, still, practicing priests.

Reese had not looked at his yearbook in ten years, and stared at the team picture: "Saints" across their uniform chests. Below the team picture of eighteen proud high school teammates—lined-up in three rows, the bottom row kneeling—surrounded by two coaches and a manager was the caption: "Regional Champs!"

"Damn, feels like ages ago."

"It was." Kay said.

"Didn't see you there."

"I know."

Reese was the starting pitcher for the Saints when they took the field for a chance to go to the State Finals in Capital City the following weekend. It would be Reese's last successful athletic moment, and why Reese vividly remembered the game and pitching so well. The weakness and fatigue did not set-in on that day. He wondered, somehow, if it could have been the adrenaline that helped him through the game. Reese pitched the Saints to a 4-2 victory and singled in an insurance run in the bottom of the sixth with two outs. He had hit .400 for the season, usually batting fifth in the line-up. Their catcher, Pat O'leara, had hit .450 as a junior and batted third. Their four-hitter hit ten homeruns, played first, and colleges were noticing them.

"Geoff Petroff. I think he went to college for a year, got drafted and played in the minors for five years or so..." Reese said to Kay.

"I remember him...big kid."

And then Reese began to think about the house parties he would go to with the guys on the team and the drinking. It had probably had an effect on his health. At least that's what the doctor had told Reese. Doctor Greene had, at least, had the decency not to tell Reese about the partying and the adverse effects with his parents in the room. Doctor Greene had, probably, suggested that cause and effect to his parents privately. Reese had been told, by the doctor, over and over, it was bad luck, and probably hereditary, although they were not aware of any their grandparents—great or not—succumbing to the same failings. And, again, it was bad luck. "You'll be able to live a normal life." Doctor Greene had said to Reese and his parents.

But, Reese never played organized baseball again. He never re-gained that kind of stamina and strength, after the operation. He was twenty-years-old.

Reese developed a sharp breaking ball his senior year, with pin-point control. More than one scout had told him if he could get his fastball to move above 85 mph, he could seriously have a chance at the professional level. His curve was exceptional and his control, truly, seemed to amaze people. He never issued more than two walks in any game he started, his senior year. Reese finished 10-1—losing his last game in the State Semi-Finals. He gave-up a two-out, two-run game-winning homerun in the top of the seventh. It snapped a 3-3 tie and the only hits and runs he had given-up in his three-plus-inning relief stint. He had had a difficult time admitting to his teammates and family how tired he had felt six days after the Regional victory. He should not have been that tired, five days later. But, by the seventh and the consecutive hits Reese suspected, for the first time, it might be something more than simple fatigue. Maybe, he should have said something during the game. But, they had had nobody else, really. And, to say he felt tired, after the game, would have sounded like an excuse. It was how they had been raised and trained as baseball play-ers and athletes. He should have been strong and ready and prepared for the game, especially with the chance to go to the State Finals! They were in the best shape of their lives and there could be no ex-cuses. They had been so psyched and ready to win! Losing was not a pleasure or an option.

"No more fastballs," he had told Coach Sutter and O'leara. He had been able to convince them he would get the last out by changing speeds, which turned-out to be a slow, straight-change and a slower curveball. Reese had gotten close enough to the outside corner of the plate—on a two-strike pitch—to get the six-hitter to reach and pop the ball to right field for the final out. The hitter had missed the left field corner with a line drive—two pitches earlier—by a foot.

The Saints went down in their last at bat, one base-runner reaching on an error. They lost 5-3.

And Reese started to feel sorry for himself, which he hated to do. The what could have been? He could not help but dwell on those games—that game—and the chance that they had as friends and teammates.

It sure made since then; sure made them smile, a lot. And the occasional school dance or house party.

"I think it was Geoff's party—after we met at a school dance—when we saw each other and actually talked for the first time."

"It was a party, wasn't it? Geoff's...?"

"Yes."

"Some of those parties were...I don't know."

"Childishly insane...?"

"I didn't like some of those guys."

"That would explain why you talked to me so much."

"You weren't as egotistical."

"Noticed you said 'as'..."

"Yes, I did."

Reese went back to the glory of his book. Or, what was, once, considered glory. He turned the page and pictured one last reminiscent glimpse of the "Saints" in action.

"Hey, you, get your head out of the clouds." Kay said; a flesh and blood reminder.

Warren was becoming restless and bored so he imagined someone reading his book: *Tales of a Sub-Urban Underground*. And, whenever in doubt, it came down to using Hendrik, reading:

> ...and the children on the street rejoiced like they were playing kick-the-can or, better yet, Simon says. Carlos sat, silently, in his pew of acceptance and final deprecation knowing he was going nowhere, after this. This had become his new life, his new community, all in the confines of this street; a dead-end street on the corner of Massaqua and his undying, mentally submitted hysteria. He could no longer defend himself of his individuality. He had, somehow, been formally beaten. And the children had gotten to him first. They had, practically, helped to conceive of him; Carlos; guided him along to gain the confidence of their parents; the adults; playing along to gain the trust of Carlos, someone different from them; someone

they had to prove to be better than; and Carlos could hear the celebratory cat-calls from the children exulting in their youth and their growing ability to conquer and create, well aware of the ceremony being propagated by the adults in The Church of the Spirtual Method: A Place of Commue. The children had warned, Carlos, not to stay in 'their neighborhood', but Carlos did not listen to children. He could hear them, now though, as the Minister of the Method fed him an 'offering' and he drank from 'the cup'. Carlos felt a chill. He knew they were watching. The street was watching through the walls. The eyes were not those of people or animal. It was of one soul; of the Community; the Neighborhood; the Street, itself, had been forced upon him. And, suddenly, Carlos felt a relief; a relief to be alive; fortunate they had branded him one of them, instead of the alternative. There were bright-white lights and white-cloth hoods draped over all the 'attendants' of the congregation, and Carlos was not quite sure why the red stain at the neck of his hood had appeared: Was it from the cup? The mark on his shoulder? He would never ask. And, maybe, one day Carlos would decide if it was his own fault he remained, to breathe, on *The Street Where Nobody Lived...*

Warren pictured Hendrik contemplating, Warren's continuing personal story analysis. Would Hendrik wonder if Warren was into cults because of what he wrote? Probably not. It was just a way to relieve the soul of its inbred insanity. Is it really worth attempting to understand what other people feel or think? Warren laughed with himself, thinking, what should or would Hendrik do at the next moment?

"Must be the mind of a writer," Hendrik thought after setting the book aside. Sometimes, life and art must imitate each other, in ironic and hopeful ways. But, it appears to be a fine line when one really begins to wonder: Which came first? The chicken or the egg? The thought or the art? Art or the action? What pre-meditated what? God or Man? Hendrik could certainly think too, Warren reasoned.

Warren read, liberally, from a book on philosophy titled: *Philosophy: B.C. and How it Relates Today*. It was another reason to allow Warren cause for amusement. It amazed him how fundamentally human these people—thousands of years ago—thought and prepared themselves for their lives with basic, healthy thinking. And with the apparent limited technology, a good portion of them could be architectural wizards. And they seemed to have a respectable life expectancy despite their limited access to medicinal concoctions and plant remedies. The air, most certainly, must have been much cleaner by today's standards. And more than rumor had it there was already the development of wine and beer, in B.C days and nights. Warren, amused again by himself and his own digressions, thought to return to his origin of thought, or the origin of life and its long-standing questions? What came first: The life or the art? What imitated what first?

Warren left himself with Hendrik, admittedly, scratching his head, probably, thinking too much. But, what to make of Warren, Hendrik must wonder? The modern world had matured and prospered in some very peculiar ways. Naivete had given way almost entirely to something darker; something that is much more difficult to pinpoint or to see, clearly; like vanity resembling something else obvious and wondering which came first? The seed? In the ground? And you simply cannot have one without the other. Too many loose pebbles in the sand and dirt of our minds to chose from, hand-in-hand, side-by-side; juggling.

Hendrik placed the book on the kitchen counter and laughed, knowing Warren as he did. *Private School Confidential* was another short story that, generally, amused him. By knowing the writer, Hendrik felt he was enjoying a much more personal insight and, maybe was able to get a better appreciation for the stories; that talking to the writer frequently—whether it was about writing or the actual stories or not—can have a positive affect on the reader's view of the story and the writing. To be able to talk too and know the writer put more of a spin to the words on the page. It seemed to give Warren Teare more of a dual personality, Hendrik thought.

"The girl in the private school—that could have been the title too—had been born, illegitimately, in the school and had been groomed and destined to teach there." Hendrik said, aloud, to himself.

Hendrik, quickly, allowed himself to get passed the implausibility of a baby girl being found in the bathroom of a private girl's school where nobody amongst the faculty or the school administrators—or the students—knew, or told, who gave birth to the infant. All assumed it was one of the students, but nobody seemed to notice a pregnant girl walking through the halls, suddenly, not pregnant anymore. The school reasoned she had been able to hide the pregnancy and gave birth in one of the bathroom stalls where the baby girl was found, crying, and wrapped in paper towels in the sink. And, being a respected private school, the principal and vice-principal—with the help of two nuns—raised the girl in the basement all through her adolescent years to avoid the bad press and the tabloid controversy. They taught the girl to read and write and by the time she was ready to start high school she had easy access and admission. The girl they named 'Mary' was content until some of the other students would inevitably ask her where she lived and with whom and some troublesome facts about her past began to be dredged-up from the gossip pool:

> "Seems strange, don't it?"
> "What's that?"
> "That she was adopted by Miss Sparrow from the convent."
> "What? Did you expect Miss Sparrow to be the real mother?"
> "Well, no, but Mary does not seem like her niece from overseas."
> "Who cares? We'll never see her again anyways. We have to go to a co-ed college and meet some men, eventually. You don't plan on staying here, do you?"
> "No." Nancy was not as attractive as Nora. "But, what if I told you I got pregnant by one of the school administrators. I think there's something wrong with the guy and I should tell someone and it might explain Mary."
> "You got all that from you being pregnant." Nora could not believe some older man would want to have sex with Nancy and she really wanted to accuse Nancy of lying. But,

there was such a matter-of-fact sincerity in her voice it just reminded Nora how easily persuaded and influenced Nancy could be. She had always aimed to please; always wanted everyone to laugh and be happy; that the prospect of being pregnant scared her less than her concern of Mary and her birthright. And, instantly, Nora felt vain and selfish for wondering why some older, married man would impregnate Nancy Dulles while never even flirting with Nora. There must be something wrong with that guy, Nora thought.
"Hey, do you want me to go with you to talk to someone"
"No. I think I'll handle this on my own. Thanks though."

And as the story proceeded, Nancy could get nobody to believe her and was accused of fabricating the story to lay the blame on some body else and not the real father. She had no witnesses, except the denial of the school administrator, of course. Nora was hesitant to testify because she was not a witness either. She had only been told by Nancy what had happened and, besides, she really did not know Nancy that well. Nora would tell herself that this would all be behind them in a few years and she could not risk her future getting mixed-up in the wrong situation or wrong 'crowd'. Nora never spoke on Nancy's behalf. There was nobody to testify on Nancy's behalf. The allegation never went to court. The private school stuck together and nobody was ever sure what became of Nancy Dulles. She left the school, presumably, to give birth somewhere else. The rumor was she had an abortion and transferred to a public school. It became know in the girls' school as the "Dulles System: Get Pregnant! Go Public!" It could be seen written on a bathroom stall.

As for Nora, by the end of the story, she was applauded by the school administrators and eventually hired to work as one of the school's teachers, earning a very respectable teacher's salary. She would work side-by-side with Mary who also became a teacher, as had been the plan for her from the start.

Hendrik and Warren continued to stay in-touch, more often than not by phone.
"I noticed you don't have any sex-scenes in your stories."

"It's too gratuitous, don't you think? Besides, I haven't had enough experience to write that shit in detail."

"Not enough experience, really?"

"And it's voyeuristic." Warren said.

"Voyeur-what...?"

"Most people don't respect that in good film or literature."

"Fuck that and fuck them."

"Damn, Hendrik, that doesn't sound like you."

"Who cares what *they* think!" It was not so much a question but an exclamation.

"How's the job?" Warren asked, smiling from his end.

"Okay. Coaching junior college baseball's not so bad."

"Be any good this year?"

"Yeah, I think we'll be better than last year."

Warren thought about the bartender from The Corner Bar. Hendrik had made no mention of the disappearance in quite some time. There had been nothing else heard on the T.V news, the newspapers, or any place else for that matter. Warren had become curious why the police had not asked to speak with Warren or Hendrik if just for the standard, token questioning. It did not seem like good police work, really—just a lack of, as it seemed to Warren. He was almost suspicious of the disregard for their presence. But, it did not seem like a good reason, or cause, to initiate this line of questioning with Hendrik and, certainly, not the police. It was times like these Warren wished his memory was not so adversely affected by excess; that his line of thinking or questioning would be questioned itself.

Hendrik would not wish to convey his suspicions about the disappearance. It would seem too ridiculous. He would not approve of what he would, eventually, be thinking and hearing.

"I had a talk with the Athletic Director and there's a chance I could be Manager of the team in three, four years—If I want it. Rimshaw might retire about then, when he turns sixty."

"That sounds rather safe and unassuming." Warren said.

"Yes, it rather does."

Warren felt like he was being mocked by Hendrik. That was rather unlike him, Warren thought.

4

Wolfgang boarded the airline after a one hour delay—briefly speaking to his parents, beforehand, which turned-out to be a practical way to navigate some time before departing the old 'stomping grounds'. He could not help but think it was a minor miracle they had never divorced. Wolfgang had been working for a law firm for seven years with most of their cases consisting of divorce and alimony and/or palimony payments constituent on who should receive what and why while, sometimes, constituting justice and fair play. He had absorbed a first-hand look at America's unbridled passion; America's staple of society; the reason for our existence. Wolfgang had never married—like his younger brother—and it was one of a few things they still had in common.

Wolfgang had a girlfriend waiting for him back home. Initially, he had not felt guilty that he had attempted to pick-up a younger woman while he had been away—for the original purpose of seeing his grandmother before she passed, as it turned-out. He had actually intended to spend one more day at the hotel he was staying, but the prospects had dwindled and he did not feel like it was worth the time or the effort to pursue or peruse the old neighborhood, anymore, just looking for a good time. Besides, he did have to return to the firm.

And, eventually, he could not help but notice his own misguided energy and wandering intentions made him feel, somewhat, like a whore.

As Wolfgang sat down in his airline seat—stuffing his one bag in the compartment above him—he became nostalgic for the old neighborhood, probably because he had had no success in getting in touch with any of his old classmates from high school. He had tried to contact three by phonebook and the thought of talking to someone like Cap Linden, again, after fifteen years might have been worthwhile. The last he had heard Cap had bought the same house he had grown-up in—after his dad had passed—and his mother had moved south to escape the winters with her second husband.

"It's the Gang-Banger!" Wolfgang imagined how Cap would have responded to seeing Wolfgang after so many years. When he had been a teenager he had started to grow tired of being called the "Gang-Banger", but the nickname had stuck because of Wolfgang's reputation of being with girls by the age of 14. And they had usually been older than him too; and the other kids had definitely taken notice. He was 15 when he had lost his virginity to a high school senior with a reputation for popularity and not giving it away to just anyone. Eva Carlotta had helped tutor him in their Spanish class and they had been as surprised as anyone how well they had gotten along.

Wolfgang seemed to remember her telling him he was her first too, which he had a difficult time in believing.

"No way...! How could you be a virgin as pretty and popular as you are?"

And she had not said much to Wolfgang after that. For years Wolfgang wondered if he had offended her by saying he could not believe she was a virgin. But, as he got older and experienced more women, he became convinced she had not been his first, but had decided to spare him the details of who had been her first. Wolfgang often wondered if he had been the first she had consented to.

Wolfgang would have been easily content if he could have heard "It's the Gang-Banger" just one time before he went back home. As much as he had become tired of hearing the semi-juvenile razzings as a teenager he would have loved to hear it one time for posterity's sake. He had almost missed it. Especially from Cap Linden who had been a linebacker on the high school football team and, in his way, was teasing the other kids who thought they were being funny and original by announcing the moniker. His emphasis on "Banger" was always exaggerated and Cap had never asked if the stories were true or if so-and-so was wild or a slut like most of the other kids would usually inquire in the attempt to amuse them selves or lengthen or heighten the rumors.

"Wow, good for you!" Cap had said to Wolfgang one time. "She won't hardly even talk to most of the guys on the football team." Cap had seemed very amused by that prospect. And he had never asked for details or location or graphics.

But, Wolfgang never got the chance to talk to Cap either. That feeling of being a ghost in his own 'old town' had persisted until finally reaching the airline.

He adjusted himself in his seat, buckled his seat belt, and listened to the stewardess repeat her monotone instruction of when not to leave your seat; no smoking; the oxygen masks will drop in an emergency; exits are two in front and two in back; and place your head between your knees. She must have done the routine a thousand times and her enthusiasm was drowned-out by her boredom. The captain's voice announced himself through a semi-muffled speaker, and he sounded only slightly more enthusiastic from the cockpit and above. Although, when he said they were ready for departure and were beginning to taxi the runway, there was a smattering of applause from the passengers.

Across the aisle from Wolfgang, about three seats away from him, he thought he heard a male, female couple discussing a "...disappearance in the Forest City Heights area..." They were not much younger than Wolfgang and they sounded like they knew what they were talking about as they compared what they had heard on the news that afternoon. Wolfgang tried to listen more closely without stretching towards them and eavesdropping, but he was sure he heard them saying a young man had disappeared after a night of bartending. And police were not saying there were any suspects, although they had not ruled-out foul play. There was no mistaking the similarities. Wolfgang knew the bar and the name well and there was little to doubt it was the same bar he had been too, many times, and had met Warren and Hendrik just two nights prior.

Wolfgang hoped nobody blamed anybody from the bar—unless they discovered evidence to the contrary. Worse yet, he sort of smiled, some people might consider his flight out of there—a day earlier than originally planned—as a getaway! Oh well. What does it matter what anybody else believes? They could not prove anything.

A sentiment Warren Teare would, eventually, share with his brother.

Liza never wanted a summer to end so soon. She was having a difficult time watching her mother try not to drink too much. There seemed to be less and less non-alcoholic beers in the refrigerator and more drink glasses watered-down with melted ice and a faint strong, stale scent that should not be present from just water or clear soda. Plus, Liza rarely found any sodapop in the fridge of any kind, clear or dark.

"I haven't been drinking any...unless its diet," Elsa had answered Liza.

What Liza did manage to accomplish was reconnect with her younger sister, who was hoping her final year of High School would never come. She had more friends than ever, it seemed, and occasionally she would ask Liza if she would like to hang-out with them. But, for the most part, Liza would not take Elsa—three years younger than her and not 18 yet—and her friends to the bars to see if she could get them drinks illegally. Yet she did on a couple occasions buy Elsa and her two or three friends a twelve-pack as a gesture of her understanding. Liza was mostly confident they would not get carried away or find trouble.

"Remember, if anyone asks you where you got the beer from you don't even know me," Liza would say, making clear eye contact with Elsa's friends to emphasize her point, before departing from their underage gathering. And they had thanked her immensely

Liza began to wonder how many more conversations she might have with her younger sister since it could very well be the last time they would share the same house and a wall separating their bedrooms. They had never questioned this, aloud, to each other but their separation was metaphysically inferred. There would be a time when Liza would not be coming back. It had happened twice already in order: Leo and then Shana. The Maine siblings were getting farther away. And it was understood Liza was next.

There had always been one good thing about their house, growing-up. All the kids had had their own bedroom. Their mom and dad had set-up their own bedroom in the basement and their mother had stayed in the basement bedroom after the divorce. As time went by, though, their mother slept more frequently on the sofa in the living

room in front of the widescreen T.V. The T.V in the basement bedroom had basic cable only and a modest 19-inch screen.

And the kids enjoyed the run of the upstairs. Their brother,
Leo, had gotten the largest room since he was the oldest. And when
he left, the girls would move about, appropriately, so that each would
maneuver subtle improvements into their new, larger bedrooms. Liza
and Elsa had the format down. Again, they knew what was to be expected of them.

"I don't know if I'll go to college." Elsa had told Liza after the
brief mention and possibility of Elsa also attending MCS the following year. "Don't think it's for me."

"It's up to you, of course. I'll be there next year."

"And, to be honest, I don't think we have enough money left to
go to school after Shana and now you."

Liza did not know how to answer, initially. She could not help
but wonder if that sounded like an excuse from, Elsa, the younger
sister who was getting a bad deal being the third Maine girl to attend
college within six years. Leo had dropped-out of college and gotten a
job at the S.I.M Plant and was living alone in an apartment.

Elsa was not sure if this bothered her or not.

Liza did not want to lecture her younger sister about, probably,
having to get a part-time job to help pay for school. And there was
always getting an Academic Scholarship.

"My grades just are not quite good enough," Elsa reminded Liza.
As the summer progressed their conversations progressed, and Liza
became more and more interested and curious if Elsa were worried
or indifferent about her future prospects. Elsa was difficult to read at
such a young age. Their likes and dislikes and similarities were slowly
being put to a test. Just how much were they alike and how important was it to marry and have children which were, basically, the un-
written rule and logical plan? Liza began to look forward to their late
night talks when it was just the two of them and Elsa, too, seemed to
have an easier time speaking her mind and being herself.

They would share with each other along with a beer or two.

"Are these supposed to be mom's beers?" They would laugh at their own bad joke because mother was attempting to be drug and alcohol free. Or was she?

"I bought them...what does it matter?" Liza concluded for the three of them. "I don't care if she drinks them anymore. She never goes anywhere anyways. It's not like she's hurting anything or anybody." And their smiles would come and go.

"When did you lose your virginity?"

"Sixteen." Liza was not the least bit surprised by the question. "And you?"

"Would you believe...?"

"Yes." Liza answered for her without hesitation. And little regret.

"I lost a boyfriend—I think—because of it."

"Fuck him then—not literally. He's a selfish prick if he broke-up with you for that."

"Yeah, but I've been having kind of a hard time meeting boys. I'm not as pretty as you and Shana."

"Oh, stop that talk."

"I can tell just by the way guys look at us."

"It's not supposed to be easy. Besides, if it's too easy you'd probably be pregnant already and we wouldn't be having this conversation." And Liza felt bad because she knew she was lying about their appearances. Elsa was not unattractive, but her face was rounder and, somehow, her sandy-blonde hair seemed thinner than Shana's and Liza's, especially on top. There was something fundamentally different in their attractive appearances. And you could always tell they were all healthy sisters.

"I don't think I'm going to age as well as you two."

"Would you stop that?" And Liza opened another beer for herself and her sister. "Next time I'm buying a bottle of red wine. I never was that crazy about beer. And light beer seems to be worse... although you're handling it well," Liza rolled her eyes.

"Why don't you just let me borrow your fake I.D and I'll get some wine this time."

"No," Liza laughed, "we don't look that much alike."

"Oh, pleeeaze doll face. See how that works."

"Besides, I don't want you getting in trouble now."

"What does it matter getting in trouble now or you or later...?"

"Oh, shush. Drink. It's my face I'll use it."

"You do think you're prettier than I am and I won't be able to pass for you."

"Do not. I didn't say that...you said that."

"The truth comes out, hypocrite. And if I do use your I.D successfully it makes you seem less attractive."

"Where do you get this stuff?"

"I'm not making it up."

"Maybe you need to smoke some more and drink less."

"Smoke what, you hash freak. Yeah, fine example you are sis... big college girl."

And they used to enjoy each other with such banter. At least Liza remembered enjoying it.

Warren was visiting Hendrik at his house. It already did not seem as new anymore. Hendrik had more furniture that included an armoire that had belonged to his grandparents who, apparently, had retrieved it from his great grandfather from the 'old country'. The wheels pointed in opposing directions and made divots on the bland, dining room carpeting. Inside the cupboard doors were Hendrik's favorite, 'old world' tankards and drinking mugs. There was a faint smell of dirty water and stale beer in the air. Hendrik ran some water through the pipes and the water flowed smoothly.

"Do you remember Jimmy LeFleur?" Warren asked Hendrik when he returned from the kitchen.

"He died in a car crash with his mom. What brought that on?"

"I never knew him that well."

"I didn't, either, except he was a good baseball player and the catcher on our 10-year-old All-Star team."

"Was he supposed to be on the 12-year-old team too?" Warren asked Hendrik.

"Yeah, I think so." Hendrik was usually better at remembering the more minute details from their past.

"Do you remember much else about him?"

"As a matter-of-fact," and Hendrik thought a moment about something he had always remembered; something that, for some reason, had left an impression on him and had remained in his memory in detail. Maybe, this was the reason why he had remembered so well; to survive in memory the respect little Jimmy LeFleur had earned in the process, "...I was at the Youth Center one day—I don't know if it was between basketball games or what—when Jimmy suddenly stood-up to that one kid who was older than us and looked like he was three years older than us...what was his name?...it'll come to me... he had facial hair when he was twelve..."

"I think I know who you're talking about. He mellowed out a lot."

"Anyways, they were picking on Norman Godette! Remember him?"

"Sure. He was a gangly kid growing-up...always likeable."

"Well, Jimmy LeFleur saw that kid making fun of Godette and just walked over to him told him 'leave him alone, he's not bothering anybody' and he just about got his assed kicked by him and his crony at the time Joey...?"

"Oh, yeah, that's right...Devdenko...! I almost forgot about him? They were like 'burnouts' back then."

"I remember watching that and I couldn't walk away and the kid had sideburns and we all swore he had facial hair by twelve...what was his name...? Saw me standing there, watching, and he told me to mind my own business."

"I can see him," Warren said, "...can't think of his name. What'd you do?"

"I think I told him I *was* minding my own business...and LeFleur just kept calmly talking to the guy, just saying 'what's the point, man, because he won't buy you something from the vending machine?'"

"That was it, huh?"

"Yeah, he told Godette to give him some change for the vending machine and I think Godette just didn't have any money on him and was probably waiting for his parents to pick-him-up. Remember that room by the main entrance where the vending machines and the drinking fountain were just off to the side by the front desk...?"

"Of course I do. We spent a lot of time there during the school year. He had a first name last name."

"Huh? His first name, yeah, it was a last name...right."

"I think by junior high he mellowed out a lot and didn't cause much trouble anymore. I can see him walking through the halls, minding his own business, in high school too...Johnson? Were there any punches thrown?"

"No. As a matter-of-fact, if I remember right, Devdenko finally calmed him down and said they should go. Jackson! That was it! Jackson something..."

"No shit. I wonder where I was?"

"That I don't know. Swimming? Open gym?"

"We did do that shit there, didn't we? Almost forgot. Battleball and basketball were constantly being played in that gym. Good call," Warren said to Hendrik thankful for his jarred memory. "Didn't Joey Devdenko...?"

"Yes, he did..."

"That's hard to believe," Warren said, jarred some more.

"Yes, it is."

"Oh, that's sweet." Liza smiled. It was the same sweet, red wine she drank with Shana. She was glad Elsa enjoyed it. They had called their brother, Leo, to see if he wanted to come over the house, but he had refused.

"Sorry, can't make it." It sounded like an excuse without explanation; nothing more than not wanting to visit the 'old house'. Liza and Elsa spoke to themselves, briefly, about how angry Leo had been with their parents after the divorce. He had refused to speak to them for, at least, a year. About the only time they saw their older brother was during the holidays and Liza and Elsa quickly realized they wished to change the subject before becoming angry with him for not wanting to, at least, visit his sisters since they had called him. Liza was prepared to say their mom was not at the house, at that moment, but she did not feel the urgency or the need to try and persuade her brother to visit. If Leo did not want to stop by she would not even suggest or insinuate pleading with him. It had not felt imperative. They had called him and he would do whatever he felt compelled to do.

"Glad you like the wine. Shana and I used to drink that."

"Are you sort of surprised Leo would not stop by?"

Liza did not answer. She rolled a small, tight joint and lit it for Elsa.

"Here."

"Hash freak." Elsa inhaled and tried not to cough. "I don't want to smoke too much though."

"Fair enough," Liza said as she opened the window by the kitchen table.

"Good idea. Mom would kill us if she knew we were smoking pot."

"Kind of ironic, she probably would be pissed. She's an alcoholic and would not approve of us smoking pot because we're too young or her daughters or for some stupid reason."

"Like, it's illegal." Elsa sort of laughed.

"Oh, don't get me started on that bullshit. Stuff should have been legalized years ago..."

Liza would call her younger sister, quite often, from Midwest Central State. She called weekly, until she used up all the minutes on her phone card—a gift from her dad. Liza was enjoying the schoolwork—which encouraged and surprised her the most—but, socially, her acquaintances became less and less personal and more distant.

She was at the Campii Moon Bar when she saw Warren Teare and had been indifferent about his presence; his college-boy, party mode, visibly inebriated, to say the least; with no apparent regard for the future, although he was attending college. He was having a good time, but she had been expecting more maturity from him and his appearance.

And she had managed to clear the smile from his face with just a few words.

"You drink too much. What's your major?" His response had been limited, right down to the attempted kiss. He had tried to convey something to her; it had almost seemed like a confessional—through his attempted smiles; something about athletics and their importance, but he stammered some, flailing, with some intent, not to finish his thought. He had been drinking to a visibly-showy buzz.

"Well, enough of that...way to serious." She had managed to comprehend over the bar music, as he held her close, dancing slowly, not with the music, really. "Good to see you, though."

Liza wondered if she should have talked to him more, but her roommate, Deena Kolish, no—that was the following year. Liza could never remember her name. Lorna Fritz? She was about as attractive and duller than her namesake; harmless, though, after further consideration years later. But, she had already met Deena Kolish and they had no idea, at the time, they would be roommates the following year, although Liza had become aware of Deena's spirit and engaging personality.

Whatever became of Deena? Liza thought not too often. She was dark-skinned and dark haired, brown-eyed, and led other college boys around by the nose with almost no effort. She was, probably, the single-most impressive free spirit Liza had ever met. She seemed to always be in a controlled, good mood without smiling too much. And she never talked about school work which had Liza wondering how she had done at MCS. Liza was not even sure if she had graduated. Their paths had crossed and they had become roommates—for that one year—and by the following summer all contact had been, somewhat mysteriously, but with incident, lost.

Liza could not admit to total ignorance, though. Nobody had questioned her sexuality as much as Deena had without saying a word. The question had been brought to Liza's attention almost completely by actions. And feel and touch. And the occasional look in her deep brown eyes. And the one morning they woke-up, together, and Deena's arms were hugging Liza around her waist from behind—and Liza had not wanted to move, but had too, as she had always convinced herself she was supposed to do. It seemed like the right thing, at that time.

It had been the only time Liza had noticed Deena and a shy—almost embarrassed—quality about her. It almost shocked Liza to see her that way, but Liza was having a difficult time talking—even looking—at Deena the next morning. And Liza had known and remembered they lay down, together, the night before, on the same bed, although they had normally occupied separate sleeping rooms. There had been no secret or unexpected visit. But, the next morning Liza was having a difficult time feeling comfortable with their new, drastically changing living arrangement. And Deena was visibly shaken by the awkwardness of the morning after and the distant discomfort of Liza's inability to talk. Liza, simply, did not want to talk. The comfort zone had been crushed.

Liza left early for a class and Deena would, eventually, go home for the summer. Liza stayed and changed apartments, again, although it was in the same building. She was hiding in plain sight and never knew if Deena Kolish returned to Midwest Central. If she had she never saw her anywhere. Not even walking on campus.

"Warren you'll never guess who I ran into on my street, so I'll just tell you. Remember the South Catholic Saints?"

"Fuckin' A I do. They beat us in the Regional!"

Kay Mannion decided to stop on their street, one day, and visit their new neighbor. Rockview Street was a long street that Kay would walk down with Nathan and Norris a couple times a week; both buckled in their stroller on large, plastic big-wheels built for two; Norris wrapped in a blanket, also, since he was not a year-old yet. She had noticed the 'For Sale' signed had been removed from the one home—about ten houses away from theirs—and decided to speak to the young man, who appeared to be about the same age as Kay and Reese, in his front yard planting some purple crocus and red impatiens. It looked like he had some hyacinth in the yard too.

"Is that hyacinth?" Kay asked, stopping with her big-wheeled, stroller.

"Yes. Love the smell," Hendrik said.

"I live down the street...just wanted to say hello." Kay continued. "They do smell good."

"Can you smell them from there?"

"No. But I know the scent."

"Thanks for stopping."

"Are you married?"

"No, never married."

"You've got to meet my husband." Kay was intrigued by a single-man owning a home, planting flowers. "He'll be thrilled to see someone closer to our age around here. It's kind of an older, retired neighborhood."

"Yeah, it is sort of." Hendrik said. "And quiet."

"That it is, for now," Kay said, glancing down at her Nathan and Norris, "until they start terrorizing the neighborhood."

"Oh, let's hope not." They laughed. Nathan and Norris seemed to be resting.

"Did you play high school baseball for South Catholic?"

"Yeah, I did." Reese turned toward the new neighbor his very own wife had invited over. "Come to think of it, you do seem kind of familiar too. What's your last name?"

"Kuns."

"Did we play against each other?"

"Yeah...hate to admit it but you pitched against us in the Regional and you beat us."

"I remember Forest City...you led-off."

"We scored off you in the first inning and then you shut-us-down."

"A single, stolen base and two ground balls...and that was you that scored."

"And your four-hitter hit a bases loaded double and you never trailed again."

"Geoff Petroff hit it. Imagine meeting you, again, after...what, thirteen years?"

"Small world..."

"You two played baseball against each other?" Kay heard from the kitchen.

"The last game we won."

"And the last high school game I ever played."

"Huh." Kay smiled upon returning from the kitchen. "That's almost sad."

"How long ago did you move-in?"

"It was a year in April."

"No kidding...can't believe we didn't notice sooner," Reese said.

"That's exactly what I thought," Kay said. "He was moving be-fore Norris was born."

"There's a baseball game coming on," Reese said, walking to-ward their widescreen T.V. "We got beers to root for the home team. Let's cook-up those hotdogs, Kay. I'll use the grille." He turned the T.V on and exited through the glass-sliding door to a square patch of cement deck where a gas grille waited to be switched-on. There was a small, round wooden table with an umbrella—not opened yet—through a hole in the center, and two lawn chairs, folded, leaning against the wooden table.

"Okay." And Hendrik watched Kay walk back into the kitchen to retrieve a package of hotdogs for Reese. Hendrik sipped on his bottle of beer and smiled at the way hospitality and coincidence went hand-in-hand.

"Reese Mannion! I remember him! He was good." Warren said.

"He's my neighbor. It was kind of funny when we realized we played against each other in the state tournament."

"He seemed skeptical at first of his wife inviting you over?"

"Yeah, I think so. I'm kind of surprised I accepted so quickly."

"She must be attractive." Warren inquired.

"I guess she is."

"What do you mean, 'you guess'...? She is or she isn't..."

"She is."

"...And that's why you accepted so quickly."

"I guess I can't argue with that. But, that could be dangerous."

"Hell yeah it could...tempting and very dangerous. They have two kids?"

"Yes. I don't want to talk about her anymore. I'll be nervous the next time I see her because we're talking about her."

Warren laughed. "You're too nice sometimes. That's probably why she likes and trusts you already."

"I might have to get a woman here for her to meet so she doesn't think I'm gay."

"She might not trust you as much if you show-up with a girl-friend. Gay might get you closer."

"But, I don't want to get that much closer...I think. They seem happily married."

"Alright, fair enough...to each his own," Warren said, laughing at Hendrik's intentions and what he considered to be right, wrong or inappropriate behavior.

"You think your ex-fling Meg what's-her-name might be available?"

"Yeah, really," and Warren laughed at the reference, "it probably wouldn't matter if she was married again or not, the little scamp." And he added. "Nothing's gonna' happen the three of you don't want to happen."

"I think that's encouraging, coming from you." Hendrik contemplated. "Plus, Reese seems like a normal guy. And then his first instincts would've proven to be right. Why would I intentionally want to do something like that?"

"Don't think so much. Whatever happens-happens."

"It's never that simple or harmless, you know that." Hendrik did not get a reply from Warren or see anything good on T.V, or receive one, personal phone call for quite some time—telemarketers, seemingly, taking control of his phone line. Summer vacation was beginning to get slow, quiet and uneventful. Hendrik, somewhat, pretended not to mind as he played music—more often than not—from the radio. Halos by the Wayside—a new band—played from improving speakers. He was not sure if he liked them at first, but he was drawn in as he listened to the female voices. It appeared there were two in the band—unless they were dubbing the same girl for the simultaneous background vocal. They seemed to make some sense; their voices and the nature and temptation of things good and bad; sex and love and lust; the way music with lyrics can, sometimes, hit home without hurting others on the impact.

"Wow, dude, I think we made a scene."

"I know," Hendrik said. "They might not invite me over again."

"Well, not you so much but me," Warren volunteered. "I'm the strange one who can't remember shit when he drinks and probably talked too much about the bartender disappearing from The Corner Bar."

"I think you did freak them out...and their other neighbor they invited."

"They invited the single mother of one to meet you."

"You think so?"

"Hell yes. Kay wanted you to connect with her. I think it's safe to say she don't think you're gay."

"Even though you showed-up, half-in-the-bag," Hendrik managed to smile.

"Was I that bad?"

"To them...? Probably..."

"Sorry."

"Don't apologize. That's not like you."

"Shit, I'm surprised I found the place now that I think about it."

"It's only about ten doors down from my house."

"Do you think Cara liked me?"

"Yeah, I think you did make her laugh."

"But, your two new friends probably didn't care for my antics."

"You did fall against a burning gas grille...amazing you didn't grille yourself."

"Fuckin' me." Warren stepped through Hendrik's front door and managed to find the sofa on his own. He plopped into the sinking cushion. "Got a beer?"

"Sure." Hendrik barely thought twice. "We're not going anywhere."

"Maybe I should have eaten something, too, but I didn't want to come-by on a first visit and eat their food and leave."

"Well, that was considerate. And you didn't break anything or flirt with Cara, too obviously." Hendrik did not look at Warren as he turned the T.V on to a sports channel.

"Do you think I talked about that bartender that disappeared too much?"

"That was a little strange. It's not like we knew the guy."

"Did I talk too much about a night I can barely remember?"

"You do seem to be babbling a bit more than usual. We saw him, briefly, for a night and I don't know what else to say." Hendrik began to wonder what Warren was insinuating if trying to insinuate at all. It almost seemed as if he wanted people to believe he knew someone that had disappeared because that would be different and even more tragic, personally. Hendrik hoped Warren would stop talking about the bartender from the Caribbean like he was trying to impress upon something; trying, too hard, to give the dead a personality and a face.

"Remember we wondered, briefly, if he was gay?"

"Okay Warren. You also thought you talked to Freddie Ford and Darius Bridgeport that night."

"Darius Bridgeport. Now he was a good athlete...star running-back on the Forest High football team and the centerfielder on our baseball team...a fine athlete. He was not that great at basketball, though, especially for a black man."

At least he's not talking about the bartender anymore, Hendrik thought, relieved for a moment. "Here's another beer."

"Not sure I should drink this."

"It's up to you."

"Play some music...How about some fusion...no lyrics." The beer bottle had already been opened by Hendrik so Warren felt obligated to drink, since it seemed okay with Hendrik too. Who was he to refuse a beer? Warren consumed and waited for some music with no one's troubled lyrics.

"Jesus, that guy sure got fucked-up in a hurry."

"I think he almost embarrassed Henry," Cara said.

"I don't think he likes that name," Kay reminded.

"He's not here."

"Should we call and see if they're alright?"

"It's only a few houses away," Reese said. "It's up to you," he concluded on second thought. Reese did not wish to argue with Kay about anything. "Funny seeing those guys, though...Warren played on that team too."

"I know," Kay said, "I heard. You guys talked about that for almost an hour before that bartender that disappeared became the topic of conversation. And he started going-on about how good a story that could make because his grandmother had just died and his brother had just left town and Hendrik had just moved and then the bartender from some island disappears and he did not have a visa so— and tell me this wasn't weird—it had the makings for a perfect crime because there were so many witnesses that came and went from the bar and anybody could have caught up to the bartender since he had been walking. 'It had the makings of a perfect murder,' he said. He seemed to be enjoying the fact he knew somebody that died, way too much. What was the bartender's name?"

"Don't know," Cara had said.

Reese shook his head.

"How long ago did you cut your hair?" Reese asked their neighbor.

"A couple weeks ago...two at the most."

Kay looked puzzled.

"Don't see you that often, I guess." She had lost some weight, too. Or was it just the short haircut.

"And he had to walk the mile from his house to work and back... late at night." Reese looked passed Cara's haircut and shook his head at the lack of insight; and the interest, retained, by his wife. "And then Warren dwelled on how close the bartender lived by him, in his apartment, not far from the lake..." Kay did not like Warren, it seemed perfectly clear to her husband.

Hendrik began to remember: Warren had gone for his drunken walk to 'wake-up' when the girls from the bar, Sarah and Michelle, had stopped by Warren's place—not far from the lake. How long would it have taken the bartender to walk the mile? He must have stopped, somewhere, because his aunt never saw him that night. Unless, she had gone to bed early and the bartender—it seemed nobody could remember his name and Hendrik was almost in disbelief, himself, he could not remember either—had left his apartment, again, to walk by the lake. This much had been remembered: There was a search along the shoreline, but nothing had been found. Warren did not live more than a quarter-mile from that same street and the small beach on that stretch of lake. Hendrik recalled seeing the picture of the beach on the T.V news. That was the last time he had seen or heard a reference to the disappearance and the only mention of the brief search the next day when the aunt realized her nephew had not slept in his room the previous night.

"What did you think about that kid?" Warren asked Hendrik, smiling, just sober enough to speak.

Hendrik could not believe Warren's timing. It was almost as if he wanted Hendrik to be thinking about the bartender that disappeared. Or somehow knew what he was thinking.

"I didn't even know his name." Warren rolled the still cool beer bottle over his brow.

Before Hendrik could tell Warren to calm down, enough is enough, he did not speak instead. He did not know what to say; did not know what to think; did not know the bartender's name and did not know or remember exactly how long Warren had walked, that night; not far from that stretch of lake, where someone had vanished; someone who did not know anyone in The Heights or Forest City, really, all that well; someone who may not have had legal access to the country let alone the city. Who would really care, or warrant, finding him besides the aunt, originally, from the same island too? Hendrik looked over at Warren who's eyes were open but barely awake nodding toward the muted movements on the T.V screen; waiting for the improvement and the connection with the musical fusion from the speakers. Warren seemed to smile at himself and, slouching, sipped from his beer bottle. Hendrik did not believe he had ever seen Warren like this. Or was it just the way he was thinking while having no-where near as much to drink?

The facts and the time were all becoming a little too muddled; a little too farfetched for Hendrik's belief. He was not the writer. He did not like he was beginning to think and feel like the detective in a cheap, dime-store novel. He only had to concern himself with his Physical Education classes starting, again, when summer vacation was over. And his own baseball season had just ended too and would start, again, in February—and the thought of coaching baseball and teaching phys. ed. had never sounded more trivial as at that moment; and Warren the absurdist observer, somehow, plotting directly or indirectly into Hendrik's head through his intoxicating-blackout over-exposure. Was it just a phase? Or something unimaginable; something never dreamed of—certainly not premeditated—until then?

Hendrik knew it did not sound like him so he told Warren to fuck himself and his overactive writer's imagination—to himself. Hendrik wanted him out of his head. All the while Warren seemed to smile, alcohol curled and pasted on his lips; still sensing yet wreaking of some form of internal havoc. The big question was how serious? And how much was understood or uncontrollable?

"It almost sounds like a perfect alibi, doesn't it?"

"What's that, Warren?" Hendrik knew exactly what Warren was talking about.

"Making people think I *want* them to think I was closer to the bartender than originally thought. You know there is no way I could have seen him...I could never have gotten back to my apartment within fifteen minutes."

"How do you know it was fifteen minutes?"

"You told me so."

"So you really don't remember that night?"

Warren smiled and closed his eyes, again, listening to the electric horn section, not a word getting in the way. Warren continued with his imagination, soaring in solos and improvisations, drinking his beer and warming in faint caution. "Besides, this livens things up a bit, don't you think?"

Hendrik listened to the saxophone solo.

"Isn't that Chic Munson?" Warren asked, not surprised Hendrik would not answer. "Didn't he overdose not long after this album was recorded?"

"Yes," Hendrik relinquished, "instant legend."

"Not that he wasn't considered one of the premier saxophone players already."

Hendrik could not help but nod, if nothing else. Warren was sounding-off like himself again. Or was that just part of the plan of the damning and the devious haling the tormented? Hendrik tried to concentrate on the fusion Warren had requested; still hoping he would speak less. And when the beat of the drums fell into place the record never sounded better. Clarity and rhythm meshed with the souls of the instruments the players had climbed within and breathed as a lifeline; the listeners finding a piece of them selves within the musician's creative, musical fusion.

Warren smiled with his eyes closed most of the hour the record played, timeless.

"So, did you like him?"

"He was odd, but certainly original."

Kay looked at her husband for clarity. "I meant Hendrik."

"Oh," Cara hesitated, "he seems nice."

"And he has his own house, right down the street, and teaches at the Community College..."

"Yes, but I have a three-year-old."

"He seems practical."

"Yes, but he didn't seem to have much interest in Carl junior."

"Did Warren?"

"I don't know."

"That probably means he showed little interest."

Reese could not help but smile at his wife playing practical matchmaker.

"And you probably shouldn't keep calling him Carl junior to other men."

At this, Cara laughed. "Yeah, that does give the impression of a husband whom I really believed in."

"How long ago did he move out?" Reese almost hesitated to ask.

"What does it matter? He had a nineteen year-old in our house, in our bed...couldn't have left with her soon enough."

"Is he with her?"

"I don't know...he might have moved back with his parents for all I care. As long as he keeps sending me child-support, I don't care."

"Did you ever see her?"

"There might have been two of them, actually...don't know their names."

"Two!" Reese could not help himself.

"Well, the one girl was a little brunette...that's the one he slept with and I think her buddy—a blonde—stopped by the house to explain it wasn't her but I told her off and told her to leave. I don't want to talk about this anymore. Can I have a drink before I go? I'm gonna' go pick-up Carl 'without the junior' in a few minutes. Grandma' probably won't mind."

Reese chuckled at the 'junior' comment and poured Cara a glass of merlot so Kay could continue to talk to Cara about something else. The merlot had not gone badly with the steaks he had grilled medium to medium-rare. When he handed Cara and Kay their wine glasses they seemed to change the subject.

"We have a proposition for you." Kay said, smiling at her husband.

Reese hesitated, not believing his racing thoughts; hoping for them to be true and that he would not falter or succumb to nervous pressure.

"Oh my God," Cara said in astonished disbelief. Reese was confident he had responded poorly even though he had not said a word, "time for me to leave!" And Cara left her glass of merlot barely half finished.

Reese concluded Cara had not lost all that much weight anyway.

Kay walked Cara to the door and they said goodbye.

"What did you think I meant?" Kay asked Reese upon closing the door behind Cara. She stood, back to the front door, looking down the hallway towards the kitchen where Reese was pouring Cara's wine into a paper cup. He swilled it quickly.

"What do you mean?"

"Nevermind," Kay said. And she walked from the front door straight to the stairwell and upstairs.

"Hey. Why didn't we go to your place the night we picked-up those two girls?"

"Sarah and Michelle...?"

"Well, yes. Who else could I mean?"

Warren was sounding more like himself as the night became early morning. Hendrik, still, did not wish to talk about that night anymore. He did not wish to believe Warren had planned a perfect alibi by not remembering and then, so openly, talking about the bartender and, apparently, that night in general.

"The drive from The Corner Bar was much closer to your apartment than to here...and considering how much alcohol was consumed," Hendrik answered.

"Oh, yeah, that was a no-brainer." There was different music playing. The new music was a little stale but it represented the kind of music Warren and Hendrik had listened to in high school. That was why Hendrik had bought the compilation. He was in no hurry to forget.

"We used to think this stuff was so good," Hendrik said. "It brings back memories."

"It does," Warren said. "It might not be all that good but it does remember."

Hendrik thought that was a peculiar way to phrase it, but he nodded at Warren's comment—remembering.

"Wonder if Michelle and Sarah would know what this is?"

"They're probably too young."

"And better off not knowing."

"Think we'll care to see them again?" Warren asked.

"I think I've got Sarah's number...somewhere."

"This music was only popular in our day...one-hit-wonders."

"Not all of it."

"No. This one they might be familiar with...*Virgin at 15.*"

"Oh, yes, they might." Hendrik laughed.

"I made-out with a sophomore at a party with this song playing."

"Who was it?"

"Does it matter?" Warren was laughing. "I think she was from the Caribbean. Her English was good."

Hendrik thought he remembered a girl from the Caribbean actually existing, with dark, suntanned skin—like the bartender Hendrik was forced not to ignore, again, fair English and all. Or had the girl been Polynesian? Hendrik felt as if Warren was continuing to play mind games with him. Warren just smiled with content.

Liza had been thinking about her old neighborhood and Forest City High School a little more than usual. Sun Belt-City College and Midwest Central State were also living, breathing memories. Together they all seemed to possess a different and modifying version of her self. And, somehow, it had become part of the process that helped return her to her 'big sister' Shana. Reconnecting with her sister had gone well. Shana would be back soon with a surprise. Liza was sure it would be worth the wait.

It had taken Liza four years more years after graduating from Midwest Central State to move, again, after attending MCS for four years. She had noticed a pattern. Four years of high school and her time spent growing in her hometown had become discouraging and she moved south to be with her sister, Shana, who then moved farther south, herself. And after spending eight years living in the same, Midwestern, college town where nothing different happened but summer and winter—and she had grown even more tired of the winters—she called her sister, again, to surprise her of her impending visit to get away from the, usual, brutally cold and snowy winters. She was tired of hoping the winter might not be too bad; tired of the winters prolonging their welcome, especially during and after the holidays.

"Jesus, he was born in a desert for Christ's sake." She liked to say to some people, knowing almost immediately if they were deeply religious or not.

And the weather in the Midwest, in general, did not seem to break down very evenly: 5 months of winter, 3 months of summer, 3 months of a mostly damp, rainy spring, and 1 month of fall; the colors and the comfort of autumn never seeming to last long enough.

"Don't be surprised if I stay. This just is not your ordinary vacation."

"Okay." Shana had laughed, knowing the feeling of accomplishing little and not wanting to fight another winter in the Midwest with borderline friends and a dwindling, separating family. It reminded Shana how badly she felt when she said she could not return for the death of her second grandfather. "Bob's still here." She had warned Liza, not wanting to think or talk or reminisce about her aging and dying grandparents.

"It's alright with me if it's alright with you two," Liza had said.

And now that was two years ago. Liza was almost always in disbelief how time passed so quickly. She had almost not realized her move to the Coastal Keys had coincided with her ten year reunion and she had, apparently, blown that off unintentionally. But, she had been aware because she had not cared really. She celebrated the holidays with her mom and Elsa and Leo—the only time she hardly ever saw her brother anymore—and visited her dad and, after the New Year, she was on a flight her parents had insisted on paying for to "get her out of town and farther away from them", Liza liked to remember how her father had joked in the airport, as they said their goodbyes. It had been the first time she had seen her mom and dad standing, side-by-side, since their divorce. And it was when she was leaving. This made her laugh too.

And Liza thought of her 'baby' sister Elsa. They had not spoken in almost a year which was very unusual. They had not spoken much since the airport. Liza was not even sure what Elsa's current address was or if she was living in the same house they had all grown-up in. Elsa was 26 and would be 27 within months. Shana was 33. She would not be 33 much longer. And Liza was turning 30! My God, she thought, I'm proof positive people do change. What the hell happened? And where is Shana? Her sister had sounded nervous and excited hoping with all her heart that Liza would not be too shocked or disappointed with the surprise. But, she had kept this 'secret' for two full days.

"Something's come up. Oh, maybe I should just tell you but I'm having more fun this way!" Shana had said to her sister. "Just don't be angry because it's not life or death if you don't appreciate it or don't see the fun in it."

And Liza could not help but be intrigued. She was, somewhat, enjoying the suspense of not knowing. She guessed Elsa was visiting but that had been the one time Shana had answered. "No, I haven't talked to her for a while either...I'll tell you that. It's not Elsa...sorry." And that had been when Shana first conceded. "Maybe I should just tell you but don't be angry if it's not anything all that exciting to you..." But Shana, still, did not want to elaborate because she was trying very hard not to spoil her 'little sister's' surprise with a clue.

"Leo?" And, as was her last promise, Shana swore not to tell her anymore. But, it gave Liza an idea because, after all, she was extremely single. What is she up to with my birthday so close?

And the phone rang.

"Hey, hon' how are you?"

"Bob, this is Liza...Shana should be back soon...some big secret. Do you know anything about what she's up too?"

"No, I don't. Tell her I called, okay."

"Okay. Nothing else...?"

"No, nothing else."

"You sure...?"

"Yes. I'm sure. I'll be talking to her."

"Okay, bye." Liza hung-up the phone. Liza knew Bob was lying, the sneak. Bob and Shana had remained friends since their days at Sun Belt-City College and he must know something. His call was too random because he normally did call asking for Shana—when she was home! She was always home when he called. He must know something. He was playing a part like he *didn't* know. They had lived together and slept in the same room together already as long as their parents had—after all the Maine children had been conceived that is.

"How come you guys aren't married?" Liza had asked her sister.

"It's working just fine this way." Shana responded. "No need to worry yourself about that."

"Oh, I'm not worried. Then again don't get married...makes perfect sense to me." It was a fine example how some girls can change and Liza and Shana as women were well aware.

And Liza began to wonder if it would be convenient to have a nice boyfriend, again. It might be hard to trust and wish to depend on someone for emotional assistance, but at least she felt she would be much wiser and quicker to the warning signs. A male companion would be helpful even if just for a short period of time; a time to learn, again; for readjustment, reassessment and for pleasure. And all the other risks and the countless variables began to persist. Liza began to feel like damaged goods. Maybe, it was time to chance it.

When the front door opened Liza laughed because she heard Bob's voice first.

"Hey Liza, I found your sister."

"I bet you did. What no work today?"

"Not on this Saturday."

"Hey Liza," She heard Shana from the front door, "did we ever tell you about Bob's brother Richard?"

"I've heard you guys mention him." I cannot believe this, in a way, Liza thought.

"Well, we got someone for you to meet."

The big secret was nothing more than a blind date.

"We just wanted to be sure you were here." Bob confirmed.

"I get it. Where is he?" They lived in a new development that could pass for mobile homes except they were not intended to be mobile. They were for working people and stood on elevated platforms to avoid flooding. There were very few retirees in the complex of winding roads that all but a lone back road had been paved over gravel. And, they were larger than most—if not all—mobile homes, although they had no upstairs or basement. It did not take Liza long to exit her room and proceed down the hallway where the three bedrooms were located, and passed the glass-sliding doors to the right—with the addition of their wooden, porch-deck that, elevated, overlooked the local, black creek, almost swallowed by umbrellas of palm trees and weeping willows. During the heart of summer, the attraction became humidity and the pulse of countless mosquitoes and purple and red dragonflies swarming, breathlessly and with endless stamina, around a sticky wall of perspiration. Not much to look forward to, Liza thought, but still better than snow and cold. And the insects did not seem to swarm and live very long; their timeline practically written on the willows and the brush surrounding the black creek's warm condensation; a different swarm; breeding; the same time, and gone, every year.

Liza glanced to her left at the kitchen-counter—opening to the kitchen—and a dining room table placed in front of two storm windows across from the kitchen doorway. The living room contained their sofa, a table, and an entertainment center five to ten feet from the glass-sliding doors. Their Creekside Manor home ended at a rather narrow hallway consisting of one closet and one small bathroom closer to the front door where Shana and Bob had retreated from the front door steps and were re-entering up the steps and into the enclosed deck from the outside. There were storm windows, all around the deck, not made of glass, and reasonably easy to clean.

Inside, there was a hammock strewn and connected from one end to the other, mostly for show; a bamboo chair that rocked by a spring from above; and a three-seat sofa that was meant to rock back-and-forth on two rails, from underneath. There was a round, clear glass table placed in the middle that was clean of cups, plates, and glasses, at that moment. The porch-deck was the common meeting place when they were not watching T.V in the living room, which was frequent since they had installed a satellite cable system.

"He's right around the corner at the car rental by the highway. He wanted to use his military card to get a discount. It's his first rental car."

"I still think he should have just..."

"It's not that much. He wanted to have his own car while he's here." Bob said in his brother's defense.

"A military brat, huh? How young is he?"

"Twenty-six...he didn't like college so he joined the military for four years. He's done with that and hopefully he'll never see any action."

"Amen."

"You know there's talk..."

"I think I hear a car coming."

The rental car was nothing fancy, but it was his, and Bob's brother could not have looked prouder as he parked next to his brother's car and appeared from the just washed and deodorized mid-size rental. It was navy blue.

"Richard Crossworth, this is Liza Maine."

"Hello."

"You're in good shape."

"Liza!"

"Thanks. So are you miss. I heard you're learning to fly small aircraft?

"Why yes I am." And they immediately planned for Richard to take Liza to her next-to-last flying lesson.

5

Hendrik needed a break; a reprieve from the lifestyle; the work; the coaching—the team was not playing very well; even the half-an-hour drive to and from work, although he rarely had to confront rush hour traffic. The only major delays were the occasional stalled car or fender bender which would eliminate one lane from the three lane highway for ten to fifteen minutes until the vehicle was towed or drivable.

And Hendrik received the token phone calls from family and friends—mostly Warren—and occasionally from school or work, but nothing that really excited much more than that. Even the usually mild-mannered Coach Rimshaw was making the job harder than it should be, Hendrik thought. He was taking the losing surprisingly hard; maybe, even personally. Hendrik was wondering if Rimshaw had no intentions of ending his coaching career with a losing record and was on the verge of saying and doing almost anything to exorcise the demons of poor play. Like most coaches he despised mental mistakes.

"Coach, I don't like to lose, either, but you're taking this too seriously," Hendrik had said to Coach Rimshaw. And then he whispered to him so the players could not here. "We really don't have the talent..."

"Don't you ever contradict me in front of the players again!" He had yelled at Hendrik afterward.

Hendrik was in search of a simple break.

"Hey, grandma', how've you been...?" He had not seen his grandparents since the Holidays and had talked to them, briefly, over the Week of the Resurrection. Hendrik's grandmother and grandfather still went to church on Sundays. They were in their early 80's and still getting around well. Grandfather Kuns still enjoyed to drive since the eyesight and reflexes were holding-up, considering their age.

"So glad you came. Come in Hendrik. How's your mom and dad?"

"Okay...talk to them every few weeks or so."

Hendrik was not in the mood for the formalities of the present. He was in search of *their* past for a while; their heritage.

"Does grandpa' still have those news clippings from the Noorsch Island Republic about great grandpa'...?"

"Of course we have those put away. I'll get them."

"Who's here?"

"It's your grandson. Help me find your father's newspaper clippings from the Football games."

"What?"

Hendrik's grandmother walked down the hallway to the bedroom where his grandfather was still questioning what was going on and with whom. Hendrik could not help but smile at his grandfather's suspect hearing; of the slow realization of what was happening; and the uninvited visitor.

"Oh, Hendrik's here. Yes, yes the clippings are in that dresser in the box. He wants to see them, fine, fine."

And it was his grandfather who brought the wooden box from the bedroom into the living room, gladly. It made Hendrik wonder why he had not asked to see the newspaper articles sooner, seeing the pride in his grandfather as he set them on the table beside the same glass bowl—that Hendrik always recalled seeing in their apartment—containing the orange and yellow and brown candy corn from the last two seasons of celebrating Hallows Eve. They were hard and probably stale but Hendrik did not remove the candy from his mouth. Hendrik looked through the glass doors from the third floor balcony and beyond their courtyard—and the empty shuffleboard course on sidewalk-pavement. Beyond, there were plenty of trees and rooftops mingling within the suburban-city limits; within eyesight and out of earshot; passed the row of assigned, red brick garages that was a part of his grandparent's apartment property. The garage space with the big, white door, opening upward, cost extra.

"Oh, dear, those are old!" Grandma Kuns said about the Hallows colored candy.

"It's okay. It's sweet and hard. Did you know October 31 is also called All Saints Day?" His grandparents, quietly, seemed to recognize this.

"I haven't looked at these for years myself." Grandfather Kuns said. "I wonder if I can still decipher the language."

"I haven't seen these since junior high. I only appreciated American Football when I was younger."

"This one's pretty easy to decipher...*Noorsch Island Republic Qualifies for World Futbol Championship!*" Most of the articles were cut-out from the local newspapers, at the time, but this was one of two where the front page had been kept in its entirety. Almost the entire page consisted of stories about the Noorsch Island Republic Futbol team.

"Do you remember that?"

"Sort of...especially once they had qualified and they were playing in the World Championships. I remember we listened on the radio from the island. It was difficult to get a reception, but we usually did. The games were played inland so it wasn't that hard to get a reception. It wasn't like they were playing south of the Equator or anything, so we listened."

"Did you notice the spelling of the name?" Grandma' Kuns asked, pointing at the team roster. "k-O-O-n-t-Z."

"Oh, yes, yes, that's right. Somebody in Immigration changed the spelling when we first came to America. That was a common practice. Looks less troublesome, I guess. But, I was four when they qualified and six when we left because of The War..."

The only other front page that had been preserved was two years older than the 'Qualification' page. It read, after translation: *Noorsch Island Gains Independence.*

"My God," Hendrik said, "they must have been proud to go from a colony to their own country...and then to qualify as their own nation for the World Championships!

"Oh, yes. Especially the way they loved futbol," Grandpa' Kuns tried not to pronounce the word 'foot' since this was not the American's game, "even back then."

"Maybe even more so..." Hendrik and his grandfather smiled.

"Would you boys like a beer?" Mrs. Kuns said, retrieving the beers, knowing the answer already.

"As a matter-of-fact it was their first attempt, and the only time they ever qualified. They still talk about *that* Noorsch Island team over there...they're praised for being part of the reason they became they're own country...which isn't true, of course, because they couldn't be playing for their country if they were not one already."

Hendrik reveled in his grandfather and great-grandfather's accomplishments.

"And here look at this article...and this one. This is who they played," and he pointed at a section of newspaper that displayed the standings and match-ups and the other Scandinavian teams they played in their Group. "Honey, WE," and Hendrik was already laughing at the mere suggestion of his grandfather's 'old country' winning and the personal pride that victory brought from that initial upbringing; and the taunt directed toward his All-American wife of fifty years, "beat *O'land*...!" And he looked around the living room, not realizing she was in the kitchen again.

"I know. I don't care. We were in America already and I don't remember those games for the life of me," and she returned from the kitchen with a wooden salad bowl filled with crunchy-hard, Bavarian-style pretzels, "you silly old coot." She removed two cans of Midwestern Ale and replaced them with two more. "You can't have too many..."

"I know, I know. These are watered down anyways."

And Hendrik's grandfather proceeded to remind him how—when he was 'not quite seven, yet'—they managed to sail to the mainland, first, then find a cargo ship that was not carrying 'suspicious' supplies so that they could ship safely to America. Supposedly, there was a great deal of concern they might be randomly torpedoed even if they were just 'suspected' of carrying illegal, wartime, cargo—but they made it.

"That's amazing."

"I can remember the tension of that trip. Not much else. I don't remember being hungry. I thought we were going to live on that ship. What did I know? It was large enough. It's hard to believe all that happened in those two, three years—at the most."

"Is it true if great grandpa' had not been on that national team you could not have gotten off the island—or the mainland."

"I think he knew just enough people on both coasts of the fishing communities—who knew who he was and respected him as a national hero—that he was able to find a way to get us over here. I think some locals on the island were actually upset with him for leaving the homeland at the first signs of war. Some felt they should find a way to defend their newfound independence. But, I think most realized Noorsch Island had, practically, no army and they were already being overrun by different Scandinavians looking to settle on the island...trying to avoid the War. There was supposedly a base for spies, pretending to be islanders, but was actually the military setting-up a radio base to detect incoming enemy ships or planes. I don't think that lasted long either. They were quickly rounded-up and probably executed within the year by the Eastern Regime as soon as they suspected there was radar on the island tracking their movements by sea and air. The Island became nothing more than a prisoner-of-war camp. There wasn't much else they could do."

"Damn. Did they have a hard time regaining their independence—after the war?"

"No. There were a lot of people from O'land and Norselande that lived with the native Islanders but not many from the other Scandinavian countries. After the war everyone just went back home—if they wanted to. Most did. Not all of course. For a small Island Republic I guess they, still, have a surprising melting pot." It did not exactly answer the question, but Hendrik could see the similarities. If you were part of a nation-country it remained to be, after the war.

"Weren't the Hendriksen's from O'land too?" Grandmother Kuns asked, knowing the answer.

"Yes. They left before the war started." Grandmother Kuns had talked to grandfather Hendriksen before Hendrik's maternal-grandfather had passed. The present conversation was all a friendly reminder. "And your maiden name was Kalmar?"

"That's right." On the occasion the two sets of grandparents were together grandmother Kalmar-Kuns and grandfather Hendriksen would recall—what they could—their memories in the same country as children. The Kalmar and Hendriksen families never crossed paths in O'land—when they were less than a hundred miles apart—and the grandparents 'to be' were shipped overseas when they were barely old enough to remember themselves. But, it was not until they emigrated across an ocean and their children had married that they finally met. They had always found that amusing and they smiled at each other because they would be thinking the same things about their past and how their families had come so far to meet. They did not talk much about it because there was only so much to say, but they would acknowledge each other with a rhetorical reminder and a thoughtful nod. It was funny how things had worked out okay.

"How long has it been since your mother's parents passed?"

"They died the same year six or seven years ago. Seven."

"I always enjoyed seeing them. They always got along very well even though they weren't both from O'land."

Hendrik smiled at his grandmother's sly—for her—ethnic jab. Grandfather Kuns paused to say something to his wife, but pointed at another newspaper article.

"Look. He scored in one of the qualifying games against Norselande."

Hendrik looked more closely and saw the name 'Koontz' scoring in the 70th minute of a 1-1 draw—on the road.

"He was a defenseman too. Look. It was a 'header'."

Hendrik smiled at the paper, reading the foreign language his grandfather was still capable of translating.

"They didn't lose a game in the World Championships..."

"Three ties, huh?" Hendrik said in response to his grandfather. He looked at a recap of the tournament and a circled section of another piece of yellowed, indoor-weathered, newspaper article. The scores against three nations from three continents were: 0-0, 1-1, and 1-1.

"Three ties, yes...only 24 teams made the field in those days... they never had a lead in the three games. But they never lost. They came home national heroes...even though they didn't advance to the next round."

They continued to browse through the clippings and the two front pages. Hours passed. Three beers consumed with his grandfather all went by and down quickly and easily.

"Some people believe the usual powerhouse teams weren't as good as they normally were because some players had been lost to the military already. Notice the Eastern Regime didn't win it...which probably annoyed their leaders to no end, in their quest for world domination. One of the Mediterranean nations didn't even win it."

"Was this the first time a country won on another continent?"

"Yes! They must have been livid, losing to—what they considered and believed—to be a third world type country who couldn't even host the World Futbol Championship—yet."

"That changed soon after the war didn't it?"

"Not long after the war was over...right, right. The first World Championship after the war, if I'm not mistaken." Hendrik's grandfather turned another clipping aside. "I wish I'd looked at these with my father more often. He was slightly modest about living in the past though."

"He must have been proud as hell about being on that team."

"Yes, I think he was. He tried to hide it though. He might have been more proud if he had played on the American team. But, still..." And they both turned a newspaper clipping aside. They stared at the black-and-white team photo. Their uniforms looked simple: dark shorts, white socks with a horizontal stripe around the calf; black shoes; a number on the jersey with a dark, vertical stripe from right shoulder to left hip. Hendrik counted with his index finger the eleven 'starters' and the head coach and his assistant coach that participated in the photograph. Hendrik wondered what the substitutes might have been doing or thinking, at that time; not permitted in the photograph. E. Koontz stood in the back row one of four players listed as 'defense' and 'fullback' surrounding the goalkeeper. It appeared the 'forwards' and the goal scorers were on one knee; first row. The two coaches stood on opposite ends. Some of the names were faded from the page, but were still legible for whoever might need to know who was who and which relative. The faces were grainy. The photograph was seventy-four years-old.

Hendrik was reminded of time again. Everybody seemed to be running out of it.

"Grandpa', you and grandma' should come by and see my house, one of these days."

"Well, we don't get around as well as we used to…"

"Oh, dear, we still drive to church almost every Sunday," Hendrik's grandmother quickly reasoned, apparently wishing to see her grandson's first house.

"If you guys want to…"

"Well, we'll see, we'll see…"

Warren Teare was up late watching old movies on T.V. He was only able to afford basic cable, so his movie selection had become limited. He could not watch new movies uncut and commercial-free, so he spent more time watching the older, black-and-white movies on the Classic Movie Channel—which seemed to bore people more than the newer movies. It was the one channel Warren felt he was actually getting his money's worth.

Some of the old movies—Warren was, initially surprised to discover, particularly the 'femme fatales'—were impressively suggestive and loaded with a dialogue of innuendoes. Sometimes, the definition of words changed over a forty, fifty year period and the dialogue lost its initial meaning and was funny for the wrong 'old fashioned' reasons. But, that still did not hurt the entertainment value. It was still worth a second-look or another-listen to see how people and a perspective and attitude could change over a period of time—like the stance of the tough-guy actor trying to 'look' the part.

Warren was enjoying the old-standbys. There were many movies, in general, that had rarely been seen let alone respected as much as they had upon their initial release. Some had become 'belated classics'; movies that had been 'discovered' ten years, or more, after their initial release and then became movies considered 'ahead of their time'. And, many times, to Warren, the movies were surprisingly good for the right reasons: gritty, realistic, location 'shooting'; deep black-and-white focus and awkward cinematic foreground shots. Warren loved the lighting. Not so much just black-and-white but grey-and-silver shining off ceiling lights and night side lamp posts.

He was, mostly, not impartial or adverse to westerns either; accommodating to the introductory scenes of the western town from the ground of its old, dirt-town road looking upward toward motionless strips of cirrus, feather-white clouds; a wagon-wheel rolling into the foreground accompanied by the cliché of a visible tumbleweed; and, with a roll and a bounce, the dust and wind escorting, bypasses the wagon tracks as the wooden-wheels clamor and creak, slowly; the wagon moving down the road as the gust of wind picks-up, grabs the tumbleweed and, quickly, rolls away and down the road—and off the screen. Warren had not watched a western in a while though. He had to admit many of the old westerns could be very difficult to differentiate—or see as original—even when they were in color.

It was fast approaching midnight. Warren turned-off the news. The news had depressed him, somewhat, but helped put things into perspective. A movie was about to begin he had never heard of let alone seen. He was mostly happy to see it was not a western. It starred an already famous actor—at the time—who would maintain a busy, familiarity well into his 60's. Rick Warsaw was a blonde who had almost been typecast a bad guy from his early roles but, soon, progressed into lead-actor and good-guy roles by the decade of the 50's. It appeared his character—in this movie—was teetering on some morally shaky ground. He was pilot for a weather station off the coast of a small, shady, southern border town called Villa Beach. His soon-to-be wife was working for a local business man who had a beach house and a seaplane docked in his own boat house. The actress was a petite blonde-bombshell of the 40's whose career would quickly fade well before the 50's were concluded. Her name was Virginia Waters. Her husband had been the director. Their divorce coincided with her plummeting career, as it turned out. The movie, *The Eye Behold the Storm,* was even more intriguing with the back story. And the other actress, Darnelle Latte, was obviously Hispanic and her name had been changed as early as a teenager to the, somewhat, exotic coffee moniker. Warren wondered: Did they have lattes in the 40's and 50's? He was not sure. And after the beautifully-brunette Latte's successful career reached the next decade her popularity, also, declined into, practically, total anonymity. She would be dead within ten years by the real age of 40! A house fire while she slept watching a movie she had starred in—as the story goes—already passed her 'prime'—a cigarette in her hand. It was morbid to see the actress knowing how tragically her life ended.

Virginia Waters ended-up working as a singing-cocktail waitress in the show-biz capital of the world—in America. She survived a total of 51 years, performing—in the end—like a 'lounge lizard' in heels; a mismanaged, misguided, divorced ex-starlet of a sideshow act. Her liver shot, presumably, working too many cocktails.

They had been young and beautiful and were gone—just like that.

And there was a storm brewing, in the movie. Darnelle Latte's character, Bethany Northrup, had been previously engaged to Rick Warsaw's character, Dak Wettland, and for some reason—that seemed to be entirely Daks's fault—he bailed-out, so to speak; foreshadowing the 'pilot of storms'? So, one day, Dak Wettland's buddy, 'Hawk', returned from a vacation up the coast and surprises Rick with the appearance of his new girlfriend—Darnelle Latte (Bethany)! And Dak—being morally troubled—wants her again since his buddy and his ex-fiancee are not married—yet.

And the ominous storm was, certainly, forming off the coast of the shady, coastal, border town of Villa Beach. Plus, Virginia Waters' character, Mary Ward, was beginning to suspect her boss, Mr. Dobbs, of exporting an illegal 'product' with his personal seaplane and the pilot her aging boss had hired to help with the 'deliveries' to Cove Haven, an even shadier town. But, this did not matter to the new, young pilot, 'Buck', who was being offered Dak's wife as part of his payment. And the 'nice girl', Mary Ward, was being encouraged to 'play along' by the aging Mr. Dobbs, limping around his beach house den with the use of a cane needed after a boating accident he had used, himself, for earlier deliveries when the company was in its infancy. And business had continued as always; growing. And the sea-plane had become necessary for the expansion of their clientele.

Hot summer sweat. The hurricane season was upon them. And a storm, certainly, was taking shape. And it was Dak Wettland who would be forced to earn-his-keep and his money to help detect, exactly, what kind of storm was heading their way. And his stormy relationships with his women were, also, right around the corner. Dak would soon be flying inside the 'eye of the storm', both literally and figuratively.

And Mr. Dobbs would need to know if he would be able to send his supply to the next 'buyer', as soon as possible—and would one of 'his' pilots brave the storm? Would Mr. Dobbs be 'forced' to hire some other pilot, using a veil of jealousy and, possibly, threats? Or could he, simply, trust the young pilot, Buck.

"Miss Ward. Would you mind going on this trip with young Buck? He'll need some assistance on this longer flight." And her boss pointed his cane playfully, he thought, in his way, at Mary and Buck. The young pilot was beginning to cling to what he thought would be his. Mary Ward could be seen, wincing, while trying not to disapprove within her modest and polite employee-etiquette.

And Bethany Northrup was on the verge of telling her boyfriend, Hawk—also a pilot—that his friend Dak was making some inappropriate calls and advances toward her because of their past. And she should not have gone to his place for a brief, unsuspecting, guilt-laden nightcap. She had left the same night, but she had let it go a little too long, a little too far, out of curiosity and their past that had been suggested to be filled with passion. She had fought him, but it was not easy. And she had seen the 'look' in his eye before she had departed. She had not seen that in him before. Not quite that intense or determined. Should she tell Dak's fiancee Mary? She would tell her boyfriend Hawk, first, if she told anyone.

And then Hawk approached Bethany, first, asking questions of a late night phone call. "Was that Dak that called?"

"Oh my God, yes." And Bethany tried to make excuses; Dak being nervous about flying into, possibly, a 'perfect' storm. He needed the work. They all needed money. By now a steady rain had convinced the whole town a storm was possible. You did not need radar to reach that conclusion. It was the storm season.

"He can talk to Mary—or me—for that matter. What's he calling you for?"

"Hank!" She called-out as he departed the room in a fury. She was one of the few who called him by his real name which, in turn, became the nickname Hawk, especially once he had become a pilot.

Dak and Hawk participated in a good old fashioned fist-fight—at least by old movie standards. It was at the hangar of the Air Traffic-Weather Bureau. The three twin-engine planes were the backdrop for their indoor brawl. Hawk—who had one two many drinks of jealousy and courage—could not overcome a blow to the head from a sober Dak Wettland grabbing hold of a crescent wrench before expending too much time and energy.

"I'm sorry, but I've got to do this. And you were in no condition to fly anyway." Dak said to Hawk, concluding the fight with the last word. Hawk rolled on the cold, hard floor and was quiet.

And Mr. Dobbs arrived at the hangar with ulterior motives in mind led by greed, of course.

"I need you to come with me." Mr. Dobbs said.

"Bug-off!" Dak had said, preparing to tow a plane from the hangar.

"Mary's at my beach house with Buck. You had better come." In his belt Mr. Dobbs may have been tickling the handle of a pistol. "We have a proposition for you Mr. Wettland."

Dak had no choice but to follow.

"You're an easy man to find, Mr. Wettland. Your women give you away." And he laughed. It seemed after Bethany was confronted by Hawk she called Mr. Dobbs's beach house knowing Mary worked there as his physical therapist. The women talked. Mr. Dobbs demanded information. And it was deducted an upset Hawk was headed to the hangar to confront Dak who had contacted the Air Traffic-Weather Bureau to investigate the storm radar had detected spinning and approaching the coast. And, being the big-time local business man, Mr. Dobbs had a hand in the Weather Bureau's local finances and its scheduling questions. It had been easy for Mr. Dobbs to find out who and when a pilot was departing. Nobody questioned him or the 'Bureau'. Not even the workers in the tower. And, like all approaching storms an up-close and personal contact was needed, immediately, by the Bureau—as, sometimes, requested by Mr. Dobbs. Dobbs needed travel information. And this was when the pilots were, truly, put to use and made their 'bonus' money. The pilots would radio back to the tower more precise information like the speed of the storm. Otherwise, they would not fly into the storms if it were suspected to be a major hurricane. But, they were not paid as well in those cases. It was a dangerous and tricky business indeed. And Mr. Dobbs had Dak coming and going with Mary Ward as his eventual leverage.

"I'm glad you won that fight Mr. Wettland. I don't think Hawk would have been up for this line of work. Besides, it's not like you never worked for me before. But, I can't chance you saying no. Not this time."

Warren was becoming amused by the performance of the relatively unknown actor playing the limping Dobbs. He was constantly smiling and enjoying him self, it seemed, almost to no end. The actor was pretty obviously nowhere near the age he was supposed to be playing but the fake grey hair seemed to improve his 'over-the-top' performance.

Dak was forced into the backseat by Mr. Dobbs, the pistol visible in his conspicuously large coat pocket. Dak did not wish to be shot. And he was worried about the safety of Mary.

"Just come with me and she will not be harmed."

The driver of the car was quiet and did not look at them or act. He wore a tropical button-up shirt and a baseball cap for the rain. He was just there to drive as Mr. Dobbs slid into the car next to Dak. Dak wore a baseball cap, too, with no visible insignia. Mr. Dobbs's soaking black hat resembled a fedora. They drove to the next scene at the beach house.

"What's going on, Mr. Dobbs?" Mary Ward asked upon the entrance of her fiancee and her employer.

"You're all going for a ride."

"I want no part of your business, anymore. I know what you're delivering."

"Too late Miss Ward," Dobbs smiled gleefully, "that's why you're going too."

The smile was cleared from the face of young Buck, Dobbs's pilot who had become easily smitten by the promise and prospect of Mary Ward. "What's he doing here? I'm flying the Seapod."

"Just remember nobody gets paid unless the product is delivered...today!"

"What about the Bureau?" Dak asked.

"You can radio them from the Seapod."

"I can't fly that into the storm. It wasn't built for that."

"That's your problem. Get the product down to Peninsula Harbor before the storm hits...into Cove Haven. We're supposed to meet three men there. Tell the Bureau what you want."

It cracked-up Warren the movie would not elaborate on 'the product'. It could have been drugs or weapons. It did not seem to matter. It might have been a motion picture 'code' at the time: Illegal 'substances' not permitted in view or description to the viewing public.

"We'd better get moving then...the Weather Bureau's already wondering why I haven't called."

Led by Dak they walked the wood-boarded pier down to the boat house. And they all seemed to be surprised—even Buck—when Mr. Dobbs boarded the seaplane too.

"Nevermind...just get this thing started. We have to be there within three hours."

And they flew low to the water, through the steady force of the rain along the coast. The seaplane looked real—to Warren—but the rain was beginning to look manufactured or super-imposed in front of the lens. Warren watched the unnecessary sway of the wings to indicate heavier rain and wind. It was easier to film from the cockpit and the coach of the seaplane. Outside the windows could be seen a grey, shifting sky. It was a set but it looked more realistic from the inside of the Seapod.

"Just keep flying to The Cove." Dobbs sat in the back with Mary Ward next to him. Buck was to the side, not even the co-pilot. "Don't worry about calling the Weather Bureau yet."

"Looks like we're gonna' beat the storm south. Coming back might be a whole 'nother matter."

"Just get us down the Peninsula to The Cove. You can worry about the tracking the storm later."

"Honey, you're not going to fly in *this?*"

"It'll be more money," Dak said. "You're paying me for this delivery and for flying into the eye of the hurricane, aren't you Mr. Dobbs?" And Dak turned in his seat toward his employer in the back of the coach.

"Eyes on the road..." Dobbs taunted, playfully waving his pistol.

"What are you going to do? Shoot me where I sit...flying this bucket?"

"I can shoot somebody."

And Buck's eyes shot quickly to Mary. Mary could not look at anyone, knowing why she had been conveniently placed next to Mr. Dobbs.

Dak adjusted in his pilot seat, looking through the steady, falling rain ahead. The rain rattled on the roof. The wind rocked the ocean below and the plane swayed, elevating quickly; and leveling.

The Seapod skipped along the water and into Peninsula Harbor toward The Cove. Cove Haven was a port town with a reputation for suspicious activity amongst its casinos and clubs and import and export business. Small boats and seaplanes routinely made the track into the harbor and the decks and piers of The Cove. It was usually busy with activity and people walking their boardwalk along the casino and club strip, but the incoming storm had Cove Haven sitting quietly—a fine model set void of people.

Warren admired the black-and-white creation of the fictitious casino-resort in this small harbor-town. Everything down to the attempt at leaning, swaying trees in the tropical storm; and the white-neon Bar sign and the white Club Haven neon sign surrounded in window black; and the use of a newsreel footage of an actual storm along an actual tropical coastline, grainier than the 'model' storm.

And Warren smiled at the detail and the ingenuity of the fake storm and the boardwalk's closed-off Club decks.

The ocean water, in the cove, in the movie, was beginning to break against the dock. Once the Seapod passed the break wall The Cove water calmed, some, but would not maintain the appearance of the storm calming inland. The waters would rise. The storm was brewing within The Cove. The boardwalk remained silent and vacant as the Seapod floated into their 'reserved' port-of-docking surrounded in the Marina-section of The Cove by parked speed boats and yachts. Most of the boats were tethered within boat houses or sheds. They were beginning to knock about in their watery parking spots. Buck got out first to help tie the Seapod to the open dock. There was no cover.

Next to them was a large boat house for a forty-foot yacht.

"We're going in there." Mr. Dobbs said. Three men stood just under cover by the large boat house. One of them was waving to Mr. Dobbs who had just stepped onto the dock, blinking from the hard, steady rain. He motioned to Mary Ward to grab one of the boxes from the compartment in the back of the Seapod's coach. She struggled with the weight as she stepped onto the dock. Dak helped Buck dock the seaplane. Mr. Dobbs hustled Mary toward the three men in rain gear and hoods, shining from the excess rain and water beginning to spray upward from The Cove. One of the hooded men grabbed the box from her and they went inside the yacht's boat house. There was plenty of room to stand on the dock-planks surrounding the yacht like a squared-horseshoe. A garage-type bay-door completely enclosed the boat house.

The other two men—and their wet, shining hoods—walked towards Dak and Buck, hands in their rain gear pockets. The brim of their caps dripped silver water from their hoods.

Dak, Buck and one of the hooded men returned from the Seapod carrying a box similar to the one Mary Ward had handed to the third hooded man. The third walked behind them, hands firmly in pockets and pointing, slightly.

Once everyone was under the reasonable cover of the yacht's boat house, they all stood on an individual dock plank. They could pretty much see and feel the light spray of water from beneath them and the small gaps between each plank. The three hooded men were in a row, boxes behind them, facing Dak, Buck, and Mary Ward.

"Okay, Dak, you can call the Bureau when you're ready. Go do what you gotta' do." Mr. Dobbs stood in the middle.

"What about them?"

There was no answer.

"What about my money for this delivery," Dak added, not looking at Mary. Mr. Dobbs seemed amused.

"Gentleman, pay him."

One of the hooded men reached deep into an inside pocket and withdrew a large, thick envelope. He tossed it to Dak who caught it, shakily, for fear of the envelope falling into the water between the horseshoe-dock and the yacht. The yacht rose slightly under its watery cover.

"What about me?" Buck asked Mr. Dobbs.

"What about you?" Mr. Dobbs smiled, intrigued by the fascination for money.

"Shut-up Buck...!" Dak was surprised Buck listened. And then Dak asked, "Would it be okay if Mary held this?"

"Dak?" Mary confused.

"It might be." Mr. Dobbs said.

"It might?"

"That's the best I can do for now." Mr. Dobbs reasoned. And then he said, "It should be." He did not smile. It was as close to a promise as Dak would receive. Dak slowly handed Mary the bulging envelope. She would not take it at first, looking at Mr. Dobbs. "Take it." Dak whispered to her, barely audible over the rain on the roof and the creaking and the bay door.

"What about me?"

"Buck, I'm beginning to think I can't afford you anymore." Mr. Dobbs turned to stare at Buck, smiling again. "Don't you care about Mary?"

Dak began his departure from the boat house. It had been understood it was time for him to leave. The hooded men had stepped from his path.

"Dak, keep going...! You've got another job to do!"

"What about Mary?"

"I was supposed to fly the Seapod. Where's my money?" Buck complained.

"Dak, leave before I change my mind...! She'll be taken care of!" Mr. Dobbs was still smiling with excitement. "Buck! You don't know when you're ahead, do you!?"

"You told me she was mine. And I'd get money."

"Buck, Buck, Buck." Mr. Dobbs shook his head.

"You were using him for this trip and..."

Dak was almost outside, but stopped in the open doorway.

"Too expensive...!" And Mr. Dobbs pulled his pistol from his coat pocket and fired. Buck stepped back, teetering on the edge. Dobbs fired again and Buck fell into the water between the dock and the yacht, hitting the hull with his left hand, grabbing at air. Buck was beneath the raging water and under the yacht within seconds.

Mary Ward fell to her knees on her plank and tried not to scream. She looked into the water.

"Grab her."

One of the hooded men laughed at Mr. Dobbs and his reaction to his own shooting and not wanting the 'good' woman to fall into the water.

"You grab her."

"Miss, he's gone." Another hooded man said calmly.

"You'd better hope that mess of yours don't float," the third-hooded man said, cryptically. "You could've buried him in your own watery grave."

"Relax," Mr. Dobbs said.

"We don't need to explain a body full of lead in The Cove," the third-hooded man continued with his business.

Dak was still-frozen in the open doorway.

"Mary?!"

"Just go Dak. But, don't ride the storm, honey, please." Her back was to everyone as she remained looking into the black water as it rolled against the yacht and beneath the planks.

"Is she going to be okay?" Dak asked, helplessly. He looked at the three hooded men. And they slowly realized he was asking them. The three looked at each other and, it appeared, there was a brief drop of the chin by two of them, maybe one; definitely not all three. Dak was in no position to ask for anything else. Dak tried to think positively.

"Tell Hawk and Bethany sorry for me." And Dak left the boat house running toward the Seapod.

"Dak!" Mary was not looking into the water anymore.

And Warren watched as the model seaplane flew into the 'teeth' of the storm. Dak Wettland radioed the Air Traffic-Weather Bureau and told them where he was, avoiding all details of the illegal activities. Hawk was soon talking to his friend, the fight well behind them. Their personal drama had escalated to matters of more importance.

"Dak, what are you doing? Don't ride this storm. You won't even make the eye! It's too dangerous! Dak come in!"

Dak stopped answering, although he could hear the questions and warnings through the storm and the static.

"Dak, where's Mary? Is she with you? Did Dobbs put you up to this? You won't make it in the seaplane! Dak!? The money's not worth it! It's too late Dak! Come in Dak! This is suicide!"

Dak would not answer again until he reached the 'eye of the storm'—If he made it.

Warren smiled at the dialogue with a beer can on the table beside him. *The Eye Behold the Storm* was almost over. It had to be. It was only a movie and would have a certain conclusion. Or would it? Warren was not so sure how this one would end. It was usually easy for Warren to predict how these 'older movies' would end.

Hendrik told his grandparents he had a nice visit.

"Thanks for the photo."

"Take care of it," Grandfather Kuns said.

"Tell your father to call us," Grandmother Kuns said.

Hendrik left the apartment planning on showing the article and the photo to Coach Rimshaw. He was sixty and might enjoy the history. Hendrik also wondered if showing the article and the history to their, somewhat, undermanned baseball team might inspire improvement; not to be content 'beating' themselves. Losing to a team that was obviously better was one thing, but to give games away and make mental mistakes was another entity entirely. It was a sign of complacency; a lack of determination and heart. And there was rarely—if ever—improvement at that conceding level of inconsistent play.

"I don't know," Coach Rimshaw said before practice the following Monday. "That was your great grandfather huh?"

"Should we show this to the team?"

"I think the only player who'd care is Peter Krecji. International football won't translate to these 19, 20 year-old kids. They're too American." And he thought about his own prediction and analysis, wondering if he had just made an unfair, biased or, maybe, even racist statement?

"I've heard Krecji on the phone speaking in his family's first language."

"Even the older kids won't show much interest. Is our oldest player 23? Anyways, I meant to apologize for yelling like I did last week."

"No problem."

"I'm getting cranking and I still don't like giving games away... and they don't seem to care."

"That's why I thought the over achieving, underdog nation might give them some sort of pride and perspective."

"Yeah, I can see the thinking there."

"And my grandfather wasn't positive but he was pretty sure some of the players were killed during the War. And my great grandfather managed to talk to two of the players from that team, years later."

"Only two...?"

"They were the only other two—that he knew of—that came to America to escape the War."

"I had an uncle who was a fighter-pilot," Coach Rimshaw whispered, not finishing his thought. He looked at the picture, again, where it lay on his desk. Rimshaw's office was no bigger than a cubicle with a roof. But, it was his. And not too cluttered with papers. "Might be a good time to tell you this could all be yours, soon. I might coach for one more year. And then, more than likely, this will all be yours—if you want it."

"That doesn't sound bad at all." Hendrik agreed—considering the alternatives.

Warren sipped on his last, remaining beer in the refrigerator. There had only been three beers left and he took his time drinking them and watching the movie. Warren was beginning to have a difficult time buying things that were not a necessity. Funds were low. But, the three beers and the movie had gone down well together; without the excess or the immediate buzz-rush. The drink and the movie had complimented each other like companions in an easy and comfortable moderation.

The model-Seapod was barreling into the storm. Dak Wettland was obsessed and on a one-way course. Rick Warsaw over-acted with a crazed look in his eye. His character was not scared, but out to prove he could 'fly this storm' even without the proper vessel. He was out to prove he was the best pilot. He did not have much else to strive for except pride and a possible 'death wish'. He had done and seen too much and he did not wish to explain to anyone why he had done so. Why had he continued like he had, ignoring? And, now, someone else had actually been killed right before his eyes. The gunshots rang in his ears; haunting and echoing, the shots rang out. He had heard a rumor, before, but this time he had been a witness. There was no denying what kind of person he had been working for; and profiting from it.

He flew higher and harder into the storm.

"I'll make it." Dak talked to himself. "What have I done to Mary?" Dak was having a flashback of introducing his then girlfriend Mary Ward—an even more impressive looking Virginia Waters in the flashback sequence; her long-blonde, wavy-hair teasing over one eye—to Mr. Dobbs.

"It's pleasure to meet you Mr. Dobbs." She was smiling, then. "I just finished nursing school with a minor in physical therapy." It had been a formality. She was already hired because of Dak's look-the-other-way relationship with Mr. Dobbs. Dobbs had the money. And now he would pay Dak's new girlfriend a fairly reasonable wage. And she practically got to live at the beach house and Dak would see her as much as he wished. And then he had seen Bethany again. For the first time Dak could see himself through someone else's eyes: The eyes of Mary and Bethany and Mr. Dobbs. And Hawk. Dak did not like what he saw.

And the storm was suddenly quiet. Dak smiled away from his memory. He had broken through.

"A.T.W.B? Come in please." There was crackling.

"Dak? We copy. Go ahead." It was Hawk.

"Hawk, I'm sorry about your head..."

"Nevermind that. Where are you?"

"I made it Hawk. I'm in the Eye."

"You crazy son of a..." And Hawk tried not to laugh.

"The storm is traveling at 120 miles-per-hour heading south by southwest. It shows no signs of letting-up before reaching the coast. You might need to bunker in people."

"Dak, where's Mary and Mr. Dobbs?"

"They should be safe down in Cove Haven." Dak paused. "The hurricane should not hit that far south."

"We're tracking with you. What are you gonna' do now?"

"I'm riding the storm out," Dak said.

"What about...?"

"I know base. I have to."

"Dak try and break through the other side..."

"The seaplane won't hold up in the winds. I'll try and stay low and use the water."

"But you'll..." Hawk could not say what the perimeter of the storm would do to Dak once the storm caught up to him in the ocean...out of gas! Dak eyed his perilously low gauge.

"Bye Hawk. I'm sorry again...for everything. It's all I can do. I got in too deep." And Dak turned-off his radio.

There was static. And then silence. Hawk did not try to call back.

"We've all looked the other way too long."

"What do you mean?" One of the radar operators in the tower said.

"He's been getting more crooked every year...anything for money."

"I guess we did suspect," a second operator said, "but we didn't want to believe as long as we were being paid."

"It's gotta' stop." Hawk pounded the counter with a fist. "Dobbs must pay with something other than money." The scene faded-out.

The next scene the storm had passed and the 40-foot yacht cruised the coastline and into the estuary and the familiar beach house of Mr. Dobbs.

The Villa Beach police were waiting; their cars lined-up at the base of the wooden pier. The sun shone bright through the openings in the sky and clouds; the colors imagined. The police lights circled and flashed.

Mr. Dobbs was the first to be visible on the deck of the yacht. The yacht was too large and the water not deep enough to dock next to the boat house. It anchored about twenty-feet from shore.

"All this for me...? Gentlemen please." The police had already prepared a dinghy and were approaching the yacht.

"Mr. Dobbs?" One of the policemen called from the pier. "Just come with us please."

"Well, I'm not very well gonna' go for a swim. What's this all about, officer, we survived the hurricane down in The Cove." The two officers in the dinghy did not speak. Mr. Dobbs seemed to limp more noticeably as he struggled to descend the ladder and board the dinghy.

The officers helped Mr. Dobbs step onto the wooden pier.

"Mr. Dobbs." The officer waiting on the pier inquired. "We've had no contact with your employees Mary Ward and Buck Wiley. Have you seen them?"

At that moment two of the hooded men emerged from the cabin of the yacht. The third was on top, behind the wheel. They had removed their hoods and rain gear. From the cabin the two men allowed Mary Ward to step onto the deck of the yacht.

"There she is!" Bethany Northrup stood with her boyfriend behind the police cars.

"Is that her Mr. Mathews?" The same policeman was doing all the talking and calling-out. He appeared to be the highest ranking official on the scene.

"Yes, it is." Hawk answered, nodding to be sure the police understood.

The dinghy went back to the yacht for Mary Ward.

"Mr. Dobbs. Where is Buck Wiley?"

"Gees, he got on the plane with Dak Wettland. They argued about working the storm...and I think Dak knew Buck was seeing his wife...terrible...hard to believe...where are they? They didn't make it through the hurricane, did they? For the life of me I don't know why they risked flying into that storm...unless Dak wanted to scare the truth from Buck...but I'm speculating...I don't know, but Dak was suspicious and insanely jealous. And he insisted he needed to make more money. I tried to tell him it wasn't worth tempting that storm. Did he scare Buck into confessing the affair? Tell me they made it. They didn't make it, did they? But, it's amazing what greed and jealousy will do to a man. Terrible, ugly business..."

"Yes it is Mr. Dobbs." The policeman said in monotone. "The Seapod was lost at sea. You don't seem too upset about losing your personal plane Mr. Dobbs."

"Oh, human life is more important than my plane. I can buy another one of those, anytime." The policeman escorted Mr. Dobbs off the pier and into a waiting police car, the lights still flashing.

"No you won't." Hawk Mathews said, his arm around Bethany's shoulders. "You won't be buying anyone, anymore."

Mr. Dobbs looked from the closed window.

"You might be surprised." He said to himself, closing his eyes, leaning back, and turning his lips to a brief smile.

Bethany hugged her boyfriend as the music began a slow, quiet crescendo. And the police brought Mary Ward over on the dinghy complete with a close-up for her to speak.

"I'm prepared to make a statement as soon as possible." Virginia Waters said, looking into the camera.

"We were hoping you would ma'am. Tell the Captain."

The Captain took her hand and helped pull her from the dinghy and onto the wooden pier.

"We haven't heard from my...from Dak since yesterday..." Mary's voice trailed off. She knew the answer. The three men from Cove Haven and the yacht loomed in Mary Ward's background. They were standing—three in a row now—waiting quietly for the dinghy to return and escort them. They stood shoulder to shoulder...watching from the deck.

Virginia Waters appeared to be walking on the wooden pier. She was not. She was in a studio with a screen-projection of water and clearing but clouded sky behind her. The actor—the Captain—was supposed to be beside her. Warren doubted he was there either. It was as if Virginia Waters floated toward the shore, walking on make-believe. The scene was hers and studio altered: A directorial intention? Mary Ward was disheveled; lipstick never smearing though. She waited for the inevitable question.

"Was Buck Wiley on the Seapod?" The Captain finally asked—from off-screen. The music got a little louder. Mary Ward paused a pained effort; floating.

"Yes. Yes he was with...Dak. Yes." And the music swelled and the horns bellowed in repetition: Dadaduh! Dadaduh! Dada-duuuh! The police Captain's response was not shone. Hawk Mathews and Bethany Northrup released from the grips of their hug not far removed from the reflecting shadows of the police car lights flashing on their sober faces.

And the credits rolled as the musical swell quieted, tragically.

Warren Teare put his hands together, clapping at his T.V screen; entertained by the possibility of someone getting away with murder; not a typical happy ending—considering the average point of view.

"That will sure make it difficult to prove his guilt." Warren said to no one.

And Warren was thrust quickly back to reality. He was not sure how much longer he could afford the rent—let alone the occasional joy of his cable movie channel.

6

Hendrik listened to the news in amazed and stunned recognition. He had did not want to admit he was recognizing the names as the pieces of the story fell into place.

"...there were four people on board the plane...the two sisters from the Forest City area...and two male companions—whose names we are still waiting to confirm—crashed their twin-engine plane off the southern tip of the Coastal Keys...and according to early reports there are no survivors..."

Hendrik called Warren immediately.

Warren had taken a late night, early morning walk about half-a-mile from his apartment to the Local Beach Club by the Great Lake. He had walked down the first entrance of Precipice Way—a horseshoe shaped street with two entrances off the main avenue—just sober enough to realize he, probably, should not be carrying a beer can in public. But, it was dark and there were not many cars on the road or many people walking, that late, on a school night. It was late May, felt like summer, and mostly quiet as Warren approached the Private: Club Members Only sign at the base of Precipice Way, a wealthy section of Forest City Heights lined with old brick homes and the, occasional, brick-fence wall surrounding a home that—fifty-years earlier—was considered a mansion. All the homes were, still, impeccably well-kept with a portion of many of the homes re-done and modernized with weather-proofing and aluminum siding. Most of the homes along the bottom of the 'cup' of Precipice Way managed long, well groomed backyards overlooking the lake.

Warren climbed the fence like he had done many times before without struggle or incident. He dropped to the other side and followed the long, not quite winding sidewalk-pathway passed three picnic tables beneath large, oak tree trunks and their thick over-hang of leaves and branches; passed the fenced-in swimming pool; the clubhouse; and down the steps to the shore; the lake's water rolling in quietly on the narrow, sands-and-rocks-and-pebbles of the beach. A fifteen-foot long cement peer jutted out into the lake—miles of water stretching-out to a barely visible midnight horizon.

Warren cracked open his beer can—it fizzed-and-bubbled-over from the motion and warm weather—and proceeded to walk the shoreline on the beach knowing it would end by a break wall, a different neighborhood, and an ivy-colored wall that may have been a hillside years and years earlier. But, now, it was mostly a steep, slab of cement wall intended to help prevent the beach from corroding below the homes that had been built above. There were large stones at the base of the wall that some would dare to balance and walk for short distances on the water. There were remnants of two, fallen tree-logs that remained partially submerged in the water most of the year that emerged as another place for local 'beachcombers' to step and test their balance and sobriety as the tides changed. Warren knew exactly where he was going, as he swigged his umpteenth beer of the week. Something drew him. Like a memory, he suspected something— pried and pressed—under a stump at the bottom of the ivory-colored wall. He stood on the break wall, looking, trying not to waver as he consumed his beer and the familiar scenery. Even Warren was beginning to wonder how familiar? Why had he returned to this section of the beach and the Great Lake again?

Warren would have strange dreams that night. He had the unforgiving image of a mannequin's hand reaching for life from the depths of a lake; The Lake. The water was dark and the hand was pale in its immoveable quest. Did it move? The lake was familiar, in the dream, as was the shore. Warren moved away from the water. And, then, the dream began to make less sense. Meg what's-her-name stood in the shallow lake; water below her waist. She dropped down to her shoulders in the water her white t-shirt returning to the surface clear-through and sticking to her torso, naval visible and nipples protruding. Why the hell was he dreaming about her? Warren questioned himself. At least it could have been a remembrance of Linda Hodson. He shook his head recalling the late night, early morning walk; and trying to avoid the picture—in his head, too clear—of the pale mannequin; of the hand's cold-white extension.

But, more importantly was the appearance of Liza Maine, in Warren's busy, booze-soaked remembrance of women and some waterside visions.

Stranger—but, not as strange as Linda—or even Meg—was the remembrance of Liza Maine and the subtle details of her face. And she had not aged, Warren remembered, in his dream. Liza had appeared from nowhere and beyond the presence of the Great Lake. She was somewhere else; appearing quietly; without a voice; and with a distant hint of a question, herself, in her blonde, blue-eyed stare. Why did she seem to be visiting and quietly asking in Warren Teare's dream? Did she have the same dreams? Warren wanted to call and ask her but that never did seem the appropriate thing to do.

Hendrik called Warren the next day. He finally answered by noon.

"See the news?"

"What news?" Warren rubbed his eyes. He was surprised how much he had drank, alone, the night before. He recalled carrying beers with him down to the Beach Club at Precipice Way. Had he taken more than one with him? He only had two pockets worthy of holding beers in his jean pants.

"No, I didn't see the news last night," he relinquished.

"It sounds official. Liza Maine was flying an airplane down where she lives off the Coastal Keys—it looks like she's gone...along with her sister and two other people on board."

Warren adjusted his phone to his other ear; a bit more alert by his disbelief.

"The other two appear to be their husbands," Hendrik continued, not able to name names, "and they're saying it might have been pilot error."

"She was the pilot and her husband was on board?"

"It appears that way."

"And her sister...? I knew her younger sister, Elsa, some."

"Looks like the older sister."

Warren remembered his odd dreams and his late night walk beyond Precipice Way; and the cold-hand; and the Great Lake looking familiar, in the dream. And *The Eye Behold the Storm* was, suddenly, more than just a movie; and Liza's quiet face seemed to ask Warren something as he recalled her blue eyes. And she blinked. And now she was gone. What happened? Warren's mind questioned; and Warren wondered if Liza would ever be available or need to visit him in a dream ever again?

About an hour later there was a knock on Warren's apartment door.

"Mr. Teare...? Are you in?"

Warren looked out his window and saw a police car parked on the street directly across from the apartment entrance. There were only two floors and six apartments in Warren's wing and the police had entered through the building door without needing to buzz in. One of the policemen was elongated and his face ridiculously rounded through the eye hole in Warren's door.

"Yes. What's going on?" Warren asked, after opening his door.

"We need to ask you a few questions."

"Can this wait...? I just found out someone I knew was killed in a plane crash and I'm going to have to move from here soon..."

"Yes, we heard that you had contacted your landlord about moving..."

"And...?" Warren waited.

"You've been seen at the Beach Club down by Precipice Way..."

"Yes."

"That's private property."

"I know. I've been stopping down their—on and off—for years. Somebody complained?"

"A body was found in the water about a hundred yards from the Beach Club."

Warren was quiet. He was not dreaming.

"It appeared to have been buried under a tree stump in the lake. Some loose clothing surfaced. Did you see anything?"

"No, not really...I think I know the area though."

"What were you doing there?"

"What does it matter what I was doing?"

"Can we come in?" The second policeman said firmly. He seemed somewhat agitated by Warren's question.

"No. Is there something you want to ask me?" Warren could not believe what he was suddenly experiencing. And, at the same time, there was a feeling of entertainment value. He was not bored. Warren felt like he was participating in a movie and he was not portraying himself. The police were, finally, talking to him. And why did he go to the lake that night...? Was he, subconsciously, looking for something...? He tried not to smile at his intuition or his inconveniently, fuzzy memory.

"Do you think this is funny?"

"No. It's not." Warren could not believe they could see that. Nothing, really, would happen for years and now he was dealing with the deaths of people he knew and a growing body count with a growing suspicion of his whereabouts as well as his method and personality and purpose or motive from the police. Warren felt he did not have any other motivation or recourse than to question and be direct himself. It was his right. And, eventually, he could see himself writing about some sort of odd triangle of lost love and death and dreams and a body that would not go away; and through the mind or the soul of a victim or an antagonist. Or however it needed to be played out.

One of the policemen was talking but Warren did not listen.

"Look. I just went down there—probably for the last time—because I'm moving soon. It's a nice walk, especially, this time of year."

"Why are you moving?"

"Expenses..."

"Were you drinking down there?"

"I had a beer with me, yes."

"Alcohol is prohibited at the Beach Club."

"Oh, c'mon...that's what people do down there...who are we kidding? I threw the beer can in the garbage." I think, Warren thought.

"I'm not liking your attitude." It was the second policeman again. He appeared to be older than the other policeman—and larger.

"I know. You don't have to ask me anymore questions."

"That's up to us."

Policeman number 1 looked at number 2.

"Do you remember the bartender that went missing about two years ago?"

"You think it was him?" Warren did not hesitate. The coincidences were becoming close to remarkable. "To be honest, I used to go to The Corner Bar."

"That was our next question."

"And I saw him working there. I think it was his last night," Warren said, knowing better.

"Okay. That was our other question."

"I'm actually surprised nobody talked to me then, when he disappeared."

"There were a lot of people in that bar that night, from what I understand," the first policeman continued.

"What was his name again?" Warren asked.

"That's not important right now."

"It's not?" Warren was almost beside himself. "I remember hearing he was from the Caribbean."

"You heard right," Policeman number 1 said, "...thanks for your time. We may want to talk to you again." And they turned and left, number 1 followed by number 2.

"Don't they want to know where I'm moving to?" Warren said to himself.

Hendrik answered the phone, this time.

"Say, I got some news for you for a change."

"When are you getting a cell phone?" Hendrik asked.

"I don't know," Warren said. "Listen. The police found the body of the missing bartender by the lake not far from Precipice Way."

"No kidding?"

"No kidding. The police were actually at my door asking me questions."

"You've been hanging-out down there, haven't you?" Hendrik asked. He was worried. Warren sounded like he was enjoying himself too much.

"That's what they asked me."

"Did they mention it being a private club and all that stuff?"

"Exactly..."

"Then what...?"

"Nothing out of the ordinary...they left. And I called you."

"Did they look through your apartment?"

"No. All they would have found were my wet shoes and socks. I told them I was down there and didn't see anything...really."

"Did you see anything when you were down there?"

"No. I don't think so. But I had the feeling something was about to give...that something might be found...a premonition or a hunch. It's kind of hard to explain...kind of like a dream I was having coming true."

"You didn't tell the cops that? Did you?"

"Hell no...! They wouldn't understand that kind of talk...of dreams or a feeling—or even a prediction—coming true. I'm not even sure you quite believe or ever get that sense."

"Well," Hendrik thought, "I know you didn't do anything wrong...I'm just wondering if you saw something down in their 'forbidden zone'—in a drunken stupor—and never told anybody."

"Interesting theory...not easy to ignore, junior detective," Warren was mostly having a good time, "interesting indeed." But then he remembered he had to start moving. And maybe do something else. He felt inspired. "I have to go. I'll talk to you later." And Warren hung his phone on the kitchen counter under the old, wooden cupboards.

Wyatt Pearce had been brought to life in the spirit of Warren Teare—as he wrote of himself—in a sense. Warren, usually, tried not to fall too far into streams of consciousness or, worse, cesspools of degradation.

Officer Craig looked at Officer Kranpool as they returned to their squad car.
"What was that?"
"What was what?" The older Officer Kranpool had been on the force for fifteen years and was thinking about returning to the gym. He had only been there

once that week. He had grown tired, quickly, of smart-mouthed suspects or civilians speaking the way they did knowing most people only became braver knowing a cop is not going to hit 'me' because they 'pay the police their salaries'. Fucking bullshit taxpayers, Kranpool thought.

"You know what I mean. The in-your-face attitude. There was no need to practically threaten the guy."

"I didn't threaten him. Believe me he'd know if he were being threatened."

"I told you to let me talk...just for that reason."

Craig grabbed the C.B-transmitter from the dashboard.

"Leaving the premises of Wyatt Pearce. No new information...copy?"

Headquarters copied.

"You know, I've been on the force almost ten years more than you and I'm sick of you giving me orders or telling me when to speak...!"

"Well, I am your superior officer when we're on the road so you're gonna' have to live with it...sergeant."

"Damn college pukes."

"What the hell is your problem?"

"You! How the hell can you stick-up for these people?"

"I'm not sticking-up for anyone...is that what this is? Jesus, Kranpool...you are a piece of work. Just because we're talking to someone doesn't mean their guilty."

Kranpool paused. "I fuckin' know...I'm just bustin' balls, some. I can't believe you just called me a 'piece of work'."

"Oh, don't get sensitive on me now." Officer Craig almost laughed.

"You don't think that guys guilty, eh?"

"No, I really don't think he did anything wrong. He might have seen something, but I don't think he's guilty of anything except, maybe, trespassing."

"Huh. No shit." Kranpool was sometimes easily convinced. It was the one good thing about his police work. He was not narrow-minded and could see two-sides of a situation when they were presented to him.

"I guess I just don't trust people like I used to." And it was not common to find a dead body in their fair suburb's reasonably quiet, lakeside community.

"I can understand that."

"All right then. Who do we interrogate next?"

Warren could not help but wonder what some people would say if he had actually been taken into custody:

"I knew I didn't like him. He talked too much about that guy disappearing," Kay Mannion might say. "I could see him being a violent, conniving drunk."

"No wonder he was so tired and not up for anything," Michelle might point out to her fun, little friend Sarah. "He was so drunk though."

"Maybe he was faking."

"How did he get there and back so fast?"

"He knew the area," Warren could see Sarah saying, at a bar, looking to pick-up someone else.

"Physically impossible...!" Hendrik knew. He must.

"Mom, dad, I can't see how he could have that night. Besides he doesn't have a truly mean bone in his body. Tell him to call me if he needs some legal assistance." And that would be his brother Wolfgang. Would he be able to help with that kind of law if there was money to be made? Could his brother be capable of taking the case for a minimal fee, since it was family? Besides, he might need an alibi too. Wolfgang had taken that early flight home the day the bartender was announced missing. And Wolfgang could hang-up his town house phone, nothing else to prove, mountains off in the distance.

And what would Linda Hodson think, for example? All those years later, she was probably married—for the second time—and might say to her rich husband:

"I think I know that guy, hon'. I went to college with him, briefly." Linda would, probably, be careful not to give her easily jealous husband too many details. "He got kicked-out of school."

"Really...? What did he get kicked-out for?" The husband would ask out of genuine curiosity; happy she had married him over Warren Teare the suspected killer. Warren pictured them watching the T.V on their kitchen counter while the husband sliced thin strips of garlic for their spaghetti sauce bubbling, gently, behind him on the stove. Mild sausage baked in the oven.

"I don't remember...maybe he was arrested for stealing? I don't think it was for stalking someone." She could say if she wished. She would not want her husband to ask her how well they knew each other. She would downplay Warren's existence as a non-physical acquaintance. It could remain her thankful secret—unless she told her hair stylist later in the week.

Warren packed some household and kitchen items into boxes. He began to think of his drive passed the two entrances of Precipice Way off Apex Avenue. Apex Avenue connected Forest City and Forest City Heights across to the next county, where the street-name changed. Warren considered taking an alternate route. The idea of driving passed the death of someone at the beach by Precipice Way had lost most—if not all—of its appeal. The excitement and the novelty was extinguishing from his once bored adrenaline and bloodstream even though the police had finally talked to him. Warren had to laugh at himself at the way his mind sometimes worked

And those dreams he had would not go away. He did not continue to have the dreams about the hand and the lake, but they remained vivid enough, along with the women. It was difficult to believe Liza Maine was gone, even though he had not seen her in fourteen years. Now it was official. If he saw her it would not be real.

Hendrik found an old basketball card he thought he had lost. It was his favorite basketball player from the Midwest who had gone east to Wynsander College, putting their basketball program on the map—if just for a short period of time.

Allan Van Meyer had spent his first five—rather unsuccessful years—playing for the River City Regals of the Professional Basketball League. The team had changed cities and names twice and, then, relocated west. After the relocation west Van Meyer was traded to the basketball crazed Bay City-East team in the PBL. The team had a once proud, winning tradition winning four titles in each of the previous two decades—eight titles in 21 years to be exact—but had since fallen on hard times. They had missed the playoffs in three straight seasons—which was unheard of for this franchise—and they were in need of a winning fix.

Season one for Van Meyer saw his star begin to rise for a high-profile team, but Bay City-East, again, did not make the playoffs. It would be the following five seasons that the "Easterners" regained much of their pride and glory making the conference finals every year and to the League's Title Series twice. It was an impressive run led in no small part by the 6'6 forward-guard who could shoot, rebound and pass the ball with equal efficiency. Some critics—and there were few—said his only fault was not 'shooting enough'. He was twice selected to the League's All-Defensive Second-Team and in the process also selected by the coaches for two All-Star games. His combination of size and speed allowed him to be a respectable shot blocker—although at 6'6 he would never be a top-notch shot blocker—and ball stealer. It was not uncommon for Allan Van Meyer to average better than a steal a game. He averaged 16.5 points 6 rebounds and a shade over 5 assists per game during his six-year stint with Bay City-East. For five years he did not miss a regular season or playoff game—until the conference finals during the fifth of those six seasons. He broke his ankle during a game-six conference final victory and missed the PBL Title Series. It would be the second year in a row Bay City-East would lose the League Title Series.

After scoring over 20 points per game for the first time, Van Meyer was not able to duplicate the same amount of success with his play or with team victories. He would miss twenty games—of an 82 game schedule—the following season trying to recover from the broken ankle. He managed to score 14 points per game, but that was his lowest point production since joining the Easterners. His rebounding totals went down; his assists stayed close to 5 per game; and Bay City-East was dismissed from the conference finals in a humbling game five loss in the best-of-seven series.

Allan Van Meyer was just 33 years-old and was traded before the start of the next season for 'younger talent'. Hendrik laughed, remembering. He had finally arrived at the age of Allan Van Meyer and it was difficult to believe 33 going on 34 was thought of as old. But, Van Meyer was not recovering well from the broken ankle and—as it turned out—he was very much near the end of his playing days in the PBL. While many believed he was overcompensating—and not even aware of it—Van Meyer tore the anterior cruciate ligament in his right knee (he had been favoring his once-broken, left ankle) while playing for the San Podres Sandmen, a team that—for years—had achieved minimal success in the PBL. They had been hoping to give their other West Bay City rivals a rare season of competition in the standings—but all went for naught. In the glitz and possible glamour of 'fun in the sun' in the west coast basketball market the Sandmen continued to lose their fans to the more popular and successful Gold State Shockers.

Allan Van Meyer's injury occurred halfway through the regular season and he was unable to return. He had spent most of the season coming off the bench as a 'sixth-man' and inspired instant offense, although there was the obvious, continuing drop-off in his rebounding. But, San Podres had seemed to improve and were in position to make the playoffs for the first time in nine years—until Van Meyer's knee injury. Not able to capitalize on his experience and the 12 points per game 'off the bench' the Sandmen won less than half their remaining games and failed to make the playoffs again.

San Podres offered Van Meyer another one year contract for the following season, but he politely declined. His basketball 'career' was over at 34. He knew he was not the same player he had been. But, Allan Van Meyer stayed in the west coast thriving without the glitz and the glamour, but hanging-on to the sunshine of the Golden State. He retired to the promise of warm weather.

Hendrik had not seen this basketball card since he was about sixteen years-old and Van Meyer had retired just one year older than Hendrik was at the moment of rediscovering the card—which had been Van Meyer's second with the Easterners and their first playoff appearance after the four seasons of unprecedented failure.

Van Meyer had just three good years ahead of him before the broken ankle in that seasons (of the basketball card) conference finals. Hendrik looked at the photograph of Van Meyer on the front of the card: Van Meyer had been 29, at that time. If he had known he had just three healthy years left, Hendrik wondered if Van Meyer would have done anything differently. The photo appeared to be a pre-game warm-up of Van Meyer shooting a free throw. He was wearing his pre-game, floor-length warm-up pants, still; Bay City-East across his jersey. Even in that first good season they had not lost in the conference finals until game six. Hendrik glanced at the back of the card and Allan Van Meyers' slowly improving statistics from year to year; from the less talented, poor shooting River City days to the start of his consistent improvement and class and higher payroll of Bay City-East.

And, suddenly, those three good years seemed terribly short. Almost like a snapshot it was over, and Hendrik put the card in a box by the photo of his great grandfather and the Noorsch Island Futbol team.

Hendrik made a plan to call his father to see if he might want to visit Bay City-East. And maybe one visit to Wynsander Island since they would be in the vicinity of the ferryboats. They had not been there since the move when he was a kid twenty-six years earlier. Maybe, when the weather got worse, they could finally take a trip out west and checkout the 'other' Bay City. But, that was even more of a long shot; more expensive; longer—if improbable—to drive. But, the climate begged improvement. And Warren had talked to Hendrik about visiting Oriental City in West Bay City. It seemed like a great place in the movies: Lots of history; lots of action; native drugs; authentic food and restaurants; and the theatre. But, that was mostly talk. Just an idea of what might sound fun or accessible like attending Wynsander College, which became improbable as adulthood had assessed. Bay City-East would be difficult enough a sell to his parents without concerning himself with the vigorous, longer and more expensive trip.

Hendrik thought he knew what the answer would be.

7

Jackson Blauser washed his face over the sink. He exhaled, as the water dripped from his chin in a mild rush, and leaned toward the mirror, blinking, to see himself clearly. It had been sometime but he thought of Joey Devdenko. Outside he could hear the police mingling in the terminal as Jackson eyed the rust forming on the pipes. The appearance of the Forest City Bus Terminal was becoming more of a responsibility. He had received his first raise in seven years and was promptly promoted to Assistant Terminal Manager. One of the policemen entered the bathroom from behind.

"We got them out of here," the officer said. "We're taking two to the station."

"Okay. Thanks." Jackson turned from the mirror after a last spit of water. "Were they homeless?"

"No. As a matter-of-fact they weren't even from around here. They were passengers."

"Oh, no shit." Jackson wiped his face and hands with a brown paper towel from the bathroom wall dispenser. The towel dispenser had lost its shine. "Did you tell the Manager?"

"Going to right now..."

"Thanks." Jackson looked at himself in the mirror again. He had always maintained the long sideburns, almost like a trademark. Jackson tossed the balled-up, soaked paper towel into the garbage can. A fly buzzed by his head and under a door to a toilet stall. The world had seemed to catch Jackson in stride, arrived, and gone by leaving him in the dust and scum of the Bus Terminal. He was marginally surprised he still worked there but change was difficult to defend. He could not see the comfort in a new work facility. And, he had finally gotten that raise and the new position.

Yet, he had not come very far from where he had grown-up. He looked good for his age but he was no longer the kid who shocked people when they found out he was in junior not senior high school. And, of course, that did not seem all that long ago.

And Jackson did some wondering of his own. What had happened to his one time close friend? And the adolescent trouble they would get into? When almost all the kids and adults alike were convinced they were nothing but juvenile delinquents? Oh, the disrespect he had shown to Old Lady Swanson. She was long gone; dead and buried. Jackson recalled his surprise how much his own mother had cried when Joey had made his final decision. And his dad had left soon after the growing suspicions. Jackson was never sure about the suspicion; tried not to think about it too much. His mother never admitted or denied a thing. She would just look at her husband or her son with little expression. She began to smoke more. Jackson could not help but think about these things from time to time.

Jackson began to sense parallels when—in the past—he would have been nothing but relieved the police had arrested transient drug dealers and/or petty thieves from his workplace. But, the homeless seemed to be bothering Jackson on a more personal level; as if they had struck a nerve close to home. He had, somehow, learned—or regressed—to feel sorry for them, over the years. Maybe the thought of becoming homeless or lucky not to be homeless had been a tormenting demon in Joey's soul. How would he turn out and was there any control? People were just trying to survive, everywhere, and there was little Jackson could do about this. Joey, probably, felt more helpless. All Jackson seemed to be doing was helping him self enough to get by with some comfort. Maybe, the future had scared Joey beyond recognition; beyond the doubts and the questions until he knew he simply could not face what he could not see.

Jackson hesitated in his own speculation. He became tired of thinking what he could only theorize.

Jackson decided, suddenly, it was time to marry. He had waited long enough. Jackson used his cell phone to tell his girlfriend what had happened at the bus station that afternoon. She worked in Human Resources for the Forest City Bus Terminal. She worked in a separate building downtown but that was how they had met—in a training session for the Bus Stations. Jackson exited the bathroom with a push of the door.

"Might sound like a crazy time but do you wanna' get married?"

She laughed and said 'probably' and they both laughed.

Jackson looked at the clock on the wall of the main lobby. It was round with large black numbers and black hands slowly did their time in its circle. It read 2:32. "Hon, I got to go. I think the two-ten is finally here." Jackson could here the commotion of a vehicle through the wall behind the counter where three ticket agents were aligned behind the raised counter, a protective glass, and a mail chute opening for each agent to speak through and exchange tickets and money. The glass cover needed cleaning again, Jackson thought. Up toward the twenty-foot high ceiling Jackson noticed a blinking light. A few of the ceiling lamps would need changing.

"Someone meet me in the loading dock. Let's get those bags unloaded and rotated," Jackson said in mild disgust. It caused two of the ticket agents to smile. Jackson was pretty sure the other employees respected him for helping with the grunt work. It had probably helped him receive the promotion. When something needed to be done—no matter how menial—he was always there to help. But, he had to admit, he could not see himself cleaning the 2:10 bathroom. The bus was late and it would more than likely smell of stale urine and feces waiting to be drained into the steel covered pit in the ground. It was not easy to get used to.

"I'll start with the bags," Jackson said. "Be sure you grab your gloves," he reminded the men in shipping and baggage handling, "this might not be pretty."

One of the employees responded with a moan. And they all stopped talking as the 2:10 passengers exited the steps of the bus and entered the terminal at close to 2:40. There were a few token "hellos" and a couple of standard welcome nods exchanged from employees and passengers. There were about twenty passengers on board and Jackson could not help but wonder if any of them could be drug dealers—or homeless. Joey crossed his mind again.

"We'll pump the gas last," Jackson said to whoever would listen. "Somebody help me with the luggage." One bag was close to exceeding the weight limit but they did not say anything about it. It had passed an inspection elsewhere so they left it alone. They rolled the large, black bag onto the pavement. They could feel the sun beating off the blacktop.

"How's Tanicia?" An employee asked Jackson. The whitewalls on the bus were covered in dirt. The bus had gone through construction on the way to the Bus Terminal and some rain two hours before arriving in the Downtown District of Forest City.

"She's alright," Jackson said. He wondered if the employee liked her. He was only about 21 and a strong looking kid. "I just talked to her before we came out here."

"On company time...?" He laughed at his own comment because he did not mean it. Jackson moved another bag into another compartment.

"Yeah, but don't tell anyone." Jackson paused for affect. He did not tell him he asked Tanicia to be his wife. Jackson was marginally upset with himself for not remembering if the employee was named Antoine or Jawann...he was fairly new. "How long have you been here?" Jackson asked.

"A month...long enough to know Miss Tanicia is smokin'."

"Miss Tanicia," Jackson repeated, smiling. Some of the luggage was not being transferred. A young couple claimed their two bags. "Antoine...that is your name isn't it...?"

"Yes Mr. Blauser."

"Thanks for the help. Call me Jackson."

"Okay."

And they proceeded to move the luggage. They cleaned the inside of the bus with the help of one more employee. There were wrapping papers and a couple of sticky spots from soda spills. And they all stood clear when the excess fluids poured from the bus and into the hole in the pavement. It splashed just enough to shake a few heads and force another step backward. Four hours worth of excrement and bile always seemed to do that no matter who was working.

"Don't forget to fill the gas tank." And Jackson walked inside the terminal to check on the ticket agents. And be sure the passengers were nothing more than safe and innocent, traveling customers.

Hendrik kissed Cara good night. It had been their third date and each one seemed to get better. So good, in fact, that she had agreed to go to Bay City-East with him to see where he had grown-up. Cara's parents had even offered to watch her 'junior' for them. Hendrik had known his parents would not want to go back even though they both had a brother and a sister that had moved back east and had not seen them in fifteen years. They both lived in a suburb in the Bay City area.

"Yeah, it's kind of funny," Hendrik had said to Cara, "we moved here thinking they would be here too, and then my aunts and uncles decided to move back. Guess they got homesick."

"Did your dad's sister and your mom's brother know each other?"

"They knew of each other...saw each other during a couple holidays. But, that was about it. I don't think they talk to each other although they live in the same county. Well, I think they're in the same county. It's not a big state."

"Do you want to look them up?"

"I don't know. I think my uncle got divorced...we probably won't have enough time to look them up and see how they're doing... not both of them. I want to see Bay City and the old 'Battleground', though."

"What's the 'Battleground'?"

"An area in the city where there were riots...buildings and cars were burned...the area was basically abandoned for years before it was gradually renovated...and some of it was left like it was as a kind of memorial for what happened. It's supposedly changed a lot...nobody lives there but there are some businesses in the area, so I've heard."

"Are you sure it's safe."

"It's as safe if not safer than any other big city...as long as you're not walking around alone after midnight."

"I'm looking forward to seeing Bay City. I've never been there."

"If we're lucky we can catch a ferryboat over to Wynsander Island."

"That would be expensive wouldn't it?"

"Yeah, probably...we'll see."

Warren Teare could see himself walking over the rocks and sand of the Great Lake. He was concerned with his own memory, for the first time. He was too often knee-deep in the lake's water and disturbing something; a brief glimpse of a piece of cloth below the surface. Warren was trying to convince himself he had stumbled and discovered something before anyone else—even if by mistake. These ideas or dreams resembled guilt, as Warren could reason; guilty of the accumulation of drink and not the tangible amounts of success that most people imagine of themselves. Warren knew he had done nothing terribly wrong. He was mostly guilty of self awareness and occasional blackouts. His soul was cleansing and appeared to be in tact. His dreams and awareness were combining in the discovery— mental and physical; soulful and visual. Warren was feeling more like himself despite the losses.

And the face of Liza Maine appeared, surprisingly, clear to him.

"Don't you think it's kind of weird your parents are going with us?"

"No. They decided they would call their brother and sister when they get to Bay City." Hendrik looked at Cara. He was a little surprised by her tone. She seemed judgmental. "Besides, we don't have to hangout with my parents, everyday. We're flying together and we're staying in different rooms...they're excited to meet you."

"They are, huh?"

"Yes." There was a mocking edge that Hendrik had not seen or heard in Cara before. It helped remind Hendrik how new he was to dating, still, and how early they were in their relationship. They had met a year before but, really, had only talked to each other a few times including the three dates. Twice they went 'out' for dinner and, once, Cara made lunch at her house so they could be with her son.

That was when Hendrik had first asked Cara if she wanted to visit Bay City-East with him.

"It will be fun." Hendrik tried to reason. And now she knew his parents had decided to go with them.

"If you say so...I couldn't take my boy with me but now your parents are going."

"I asked them if they wanted to go."

"Before me...?"

"Yes. Your boy's only three. He wouldn't appreciate this trip."

"That's not that young. Besides, this was supposed to be our trip."

"No. This was my idea for a trip and I wanted to go with my parents. Then I asked you."

"Maybe you should just go with mom and dad."

Hendrik was surprised she had not phrased it "mommy and daddy". He looked at Cara who would not do the same. "You might like them. I was surprised they called back and said they would go too, but I wasn't going to tell them they couldn't go. That was up to them."

"Okay. I know." Cara looked at Hendrik. "I've been avoiding my ex's parents and I'm just not excited about traveling with yours." And she stopped; hearing herself. "And that's not fair to you or your parents."

"So, you're still goin'?"

"Yeah, I guess," Cara said, "if you want me?"

"I do." Hendrik felt himself smile. "Good."

Warren did not want to move but he had little choice in the matter. Economics would not allow him to live on his own. And the writing was not paying for anything on its own. The short stories had become nothing more than a show piece of no additional value. He had to write something else and he needed a space where rent was not a necessity. Warren had found a place but it embarrassed him to tell people where he was moving to—again. It was a step back but, at least, the police had stopped calling to interview him. One policeman asked him to "come down to the station" but Warren had politely declined, at first. When he remembered he was about to have a change of address he did stop at the police station and they talked for about an hour about who was at The Corner Bar the night the bartender from the Caribbean Islands disappeared. And somebody finally said the bartender's name was Jonah. And Warren smiled because he finally knew the bartender's name and he would not forget it, this time.

"You should have a talk with Hendrik Kuns. He'll probably have a better recollection of the entire night than I do," Warren had told the police upon departing.

"Thanks. We'll do that."

"Or did we talk to him already?" Warren heard one of the other detectives say as Warren exited the room. They had been sitting on wooden chairs and leaning on a large round table that might have been used in a high school cafeteria.

And Warren was gone from the police station hopeful of never returning. He would probably call Hendrik, soon, to see if the police had talked to him.

There was not much else left for Warren to do. He wished he could go find a pick-up, fast pitch baseball game with the old neighborhood like they used to when he and Hendrik first started hanging-out together when they were seven and eight-years-old; and, then, the first hardball team when they were on the Red Leopards; and Junior High School; and Varsity High School baseball. They had been pretty good; and then the minor fiasco at Midwest Central State. He had been proud of making the baseball team; surprised they had told him they wanted him to play third base—and pitch some! He could throw in the low to mid 80's and he honestly believed he could not throw hard enough to pitch at the college level. But, the coaches told him they wanted to "give him a look". Warren was more proud of that than making the basketball team. He knew he would have barely played on the basketball team, anyways, but he had a chance for plenty of action playing baseball for the "Hillsiders" of Midwest Central State.

There were no mountains around Midwest Central but there were plenty of green, rolling hillsides around the campus—south and eastward—with woods and forests along the highway for ten and twenty mile stretches. It was a pleasant drive in and around the campus of MCS. Warren had been proud—if only briefly—and almost worthy of being a Midwest Central State Hillsider.

Warren realized he had to write some more, even if it got him nowhere. It was something he could do and should. There were plenty of thoughts in his head that he did not need or wish to forget by way of life—in general—or drink or blackouts. Warren began to recall, more and more, now that she was gone, Liza Maine and their not so distant past together. They had known each other well during their days at Forest City High School: 'The Heights'. He recalled the day she was almost in tears, realizing:

"What if we don't see each other after graduation...what's gonna' happen?"

They had been alone together and Warren remembered drinking from his beer can and kissing her on the cheek and she lay her head on his shoulder. Some music played fairly loudly on the radio and there were a few kids walking around the house of a small get-together; in someone's house Warren, briefly, could not remember. Hendrik had been there too. They had been at Hendrik's house when his parents had taken a rare trip east to visit family for a week. Warren had put his beer down and put his arms around Liza and they had kissed for the second and third time. He had not liked the idea of them not seeing each other after graduating from high school, but he never admitted that to Liza; he could never have realized how right she would be. From the radio a song sang to them—or, maybe, it just meant more to Warren, looking back, remembering the song that happened to be playing as he sat with Liza, at that moment: "...in the wink of a young girl's eye/oh those days/bright and gone..."

Warren planned to write another book. This time it would not be short stories, but something novel. It did not take long for Warren to see the length and who the main character should be; or who he wanted her to be. Warren wrote the title down just to be sure it remained fresh in his memory. He hoped to pay homage and he hoped not to offend—unless he had to. He thought about changing her name for the book, since, in reality, the book would be fiction. Warren, initially, wrote the title out this way: *The Passing of Liza Maine*. And, for the first time in quite some time Warren felt the need to complete something; a need almost like a craving or an addiction without the excess. It began to feel like the creative makings of cause and affect; something less complicated and much healthier, in the long run.

Warren Teare's vision of the book was clear. And he planned never to spell that out; that it, certainly, would be honest and simply realized—even if nobody read it.

www.ingramcontent.com/pod-product-compliance
Lightning Source LLC
Chambersburg PA
CBHW071345170626
46811CB00003B/998